Cold Enough for Snow

Jessica Au

COLD ENOUGH FOR SNOW

A NEW DIRECTIONS
PAPERBOOK ORIGINAL

Published simultaneously by New Directions in the United States,
Fitzcarraldo in the United Kingdom,
and Giramondo in Australia

This novel has been assisted by the Australian Government
through the Australia Council, its arts funding and advisory body,
and by the Victorian Government through Creative Victoria

Manufactured in the United States of America
First published as a New Directions Paperbook (NDP1522) in 2022
Design by Erik Rieselbach

Library of Congress Cataloging-in-Publication Data
Names: Au, Jessica, author.
Title: Cold enough for snow / Jessica Au.
Description: First New Directions edition. |
New York : New Directions Publishing Corporation, 2022.
Identifiers: LCCN 2021046197 | ISBN 9780811231558 (paperback) |
ISBN 9780811231565 (ebook)
Subjects: LCSH: Mothers and daughters—Fiction. |
LCGFT: Domestic fiction. | Novels.
Classification: LCC PR9619.4.A93 C65 2022 | DDC 823/.92—dc23
LC record available at https://lccn.loc.gov/2021046197

6 8 10 9 7

New Directions Books are published for James Laughlin
by New Directions Publishing Corporation
80 Eighth Avenue, New York 10011

for Oliver

When we left the hotel it was raining, a light, fine rain, as can sometimes happen in Tokyo in October. I said that where we were going was not far—we would only need to get to the station, the same one that we had arrived at yesterday, and then catch two trains and walk a little down some small streets until we got to the museum. I got out my umbrella and opened it, and pulled up the zipper of my coat. It was early morning and the street was filled with people, most walking away from the station, rather than toward it as we were. All the while, my mother stayed close to me, as if she felt that the flow of the crowd was a current, and that if we were separated, we would not be able to make our way back to each other, but continue to drift further and further apart. The rain was gentle, and consistent. It left a fine layer of water on the ground, which was not asphalt, but a series of small, square tiles, if you cared enough to notice.

We had arrived the night before. My plane landed an hour before my mother's and I waited for her at the airport. I was too tired to read but collected my bags and bought us two tickets for one of the express trains, as well as a bottle of water and some cash from the ATM. I wondered if I should buy more—some tea perhaps, or something to eat, but I did not know how she would be feeling when she landed. When she came out of the doors, I recognized her immediately, even from a distance, somehow by the way she held herself or the way she walked, without being able to clearly see her face. Up close, I noticed that she continued to dress with care: a brown shirt with pearl buttons, tailored pants and small items of jade. It had always been that way. Her clothes were not expensive, but were chosen with attention to the cut and fit, the subtle combination of textures. She looked like a well-dressed woman in a movie from maybe twenty or thirty years ago, both dated and elegant. I saw too that she had with her a large suitcase, the same one I remembered from our childhood. She'd kept it on top of the cupboard in her room, where it had loomed over us, mostly unused, only brought down for the few trips she'd made back to Hong Kong, like for when her father died, and then her brother. There was hardly a mark on it, and even now, it seemed almost new.

Earlier in the year, I had asked her to come with me on a trip to Japan. We did not live in the same city anymore, and had never really been away together as adults, but I was beginning to feel that it was important, for reasons I could not yet name. At first, she had been reluctant, but I had pushed, and eventually she had agreed, not in so many words, but by protesting slightly less, or hesitating over the phone when I asked her, and by those acts alone, I knew that she was finally signaling that she would come. I had chosen Japan because I had been there before, and although my mother had not, I thought she might be more at ease exploring another part of Asia. And perhaps I felt that this would put us on equal footing in some way, to both be made strangers. I had decided on autumn, because it had always been our favorite season. The gardens and parks would be at their most beautiful then; the late season, everything almost gone. I had not anticipated that it might still be a time for typhoons. Already, the weather reports had contained several warnings, and it had been raining steadily since our arrival.

At the station, I gave my mother her metro card and we passed through the turnstiles. Inside, I searched for the train line and platform that we needed, trying to match the name and colors to what I had marked on the map the night before. Eventually, I found the right connection. On the platform, the ground had been marked to indicate where you could line up to board. We took our place obediently and the train arrived within minutes. There was a single spare seat close to the door, and I indicated that she should sit, while I stood next to her and watched as the stations passed us by. The city was gray and concrete, dull in the rain and not entirely unfamiliar. I recognized the form of everything—buildings, overpasses, train crossings—but in their details, their materials, they were all slightly different, and it was these small but significant changes that continued to absorb me. After about twenty minutes, we switched to a smaller line and a less crowded train, and this time I was able to sit next to her, watching as the height of the buildings grew lower and lower, until we were in the suburbs, and they became homes, with white walls and flat roofs and compact cars parked in the driveways. It struck me that the last time I had been here, I was with Laurie, and thinking on and off about my mother. And now, I was here with her, thinking on and off about him, about how we had rushed around the city from morning to long after dark, seeing everything, taking in everything. During that trip, it was like we were children again, mad and excitable, endlessly talking, endlessly laughing, always hungry for more. I remembered thinking that I had wanted to share some of this with my mother, even if just a small amount. It was after that trip that I had begun learning Japanese, as if subconsciously planning for this journey.

Our exit this time was on a quiet street in a leafy neighborhood. Many of the houses were built right up to the road, but people had placed small planters in what little space there was, with peonies or bonsai. We too had had a bonsai when I was growing up, in a white square pot with tiny feet. I don't think my mother would have bought one, so it must have been a gift that we kept and tended for a very long time. For some reason, I remembered disliking it as a child. Perhaps because I thought it looked unnatural,

3

or lonely, this very detailed, tiny tree, almost like an illustration, growing alone when it looked like it should have been in a forest.

As we walked, we passed by a building with a wall of translucent glass bricks, and another whose surface was the color of mushrooms. Ahead of us, a woman was sweeping some leaves up from the street and putting them in a bag. We spoke for a while about my mother's new flat, which I had not yet seen. She had recently left our childhood home and moved to a small building in the outer suburbs, which was nearer to where my sister lived, and closer to her grandchildren. I asked her if she liked it there, if there were the right shops so that she could buy the food she liked, if her friends were near. She said that the birds in the morning were very loud. She had thought at first they were children screaming and had gone outside to try and listen better, to check if everything was okay. Then she had realized that the sound was birds, but when she looked for them in the trees, she had not seen them. Out there, there were big blocks of land, freeways. You could walk and walk and not see anyone, despite all the houses around you.

I noticed that there was a park coming up ahead and checked the map on my phone. I said to my mother that we should go through it, the distance to the museum would be about the same. Somewhere along the way, it had stopped raining and we lowered our umbrellas. Inside, the park was vast, with a dark canopy and winding paths. It was the way I had imagined parks to be in my childhood, wooded and dim and wet, a world within a world. We passed an empty playground, with a metal slide with blue metal edges, whose surface still held big, fat drops of rain. A series of small streams wound their way through the trees and crossed and separated and crossed one another again. Flat stones broke the water, like tiny gorges or mountains, and here and there were small, narrow bridges, the kind you often saw in postcards or travel shots of the East.

Before leaving, I had bought a new camera, a Nikon. Though digital, it had three small dials and a glass viewfinder, as well as a short lens that you could turn with your fingers to adjust the aperture. It reminded me of the camera my uncle had used to take family photos during their youth in Hong Kong. My mother still had some of these images. I'd looked at them often as a child, listening to the stories that went with them, fascinated by the spots of color that sometimes caught there, like a drop of oil in water, burning a bright hole in the surface. To me the photographs seemed to have an old-world elegance about them, with my mother and uncle posed almost like a traditional husband and wife, she seated and he standing behind her shoulder, their hair set in a certain way, wearing a patterned dress or pressed white shirt, with the streets and skies of Hong Kong looking sultry and wet behind them. After a while, I forgot completely about these photos, and only discovered them again years later when my sister and I were cleaning everything out of my mother's flat, in a shoebox filled with yellow envelopes and small albums.

I took out the camera now, adjusted the exposure, and fell back with my eye to the viewfinder. My mother, sensing the change in the distance between us, turned and saw what I was doing. Immediately, she assumed a stock pose: feet together, back straight, hands clasped. Is this all right, she asked me, or should I stand over there, nearer to that tree? Actually, I had wanted to catch something different, to see her face as it was during ordinary time, when she was alone with her thoughts, but I said it looked good and took the photo anyway. She asked if she should take one of me, but I said no, that we had better move on.

In the weeks leading up to the trip, I had spent many hours searching various places—shrines, wooded parks, galleries, the few old houses left after the war—thinking all the while of what she might like to see. I had saved a large file on my laptop with addresses, descriptions and opening times, adding and subtracting many things, worrying over the correct balance, wanting to make the most of our time here. The museum had been recommended by a friend. It was part of a large prewar house that had been built by a famous sculptor. I had read a lot about the house online, and was looking forward to seeing it. I checked my phone again and said that if we turned here, we'd soon get to the street where the museum was located. As we walked, I explained to my mother a little of what to expect, being careful not to give away too much detail, to leave things to be discovered.

On the way, we passed by the gates of a school where children were having their morning break. They wore small colored hats to show perhaps their age or grade, and were playing loudly and freely. The school grounds were clean and the play equipment bright, and several teachers stood around, watching them calmly. I thought, and wondered if my mother thought too, of the Catholic school she had enrolled us in, not exactly for the quality of the education, but because of the plaid wool skirts and blue Bibles and experiences such as these, all the things she had been taught to think of and want for herself. After a few years there, both my sister and I won scholarships and stayed on till the end of high school, eventually graduating and going on to university: my sister to study medicine, and I, English literature.

At the museum entrance, there was a stand where you could clip your umbrella, presumably so that you would not track water through the old house. I took my mother's, shook it out a little, and put both of ours next to each other, pocketing the little keys so we could retrieve them later. Inside, past the sliding doors, there was a designated space for you to remove your shoes, with two wooden stools, and baskets full of brown slippers. While I struggled with my boots, my mother, I noticed, slipped off hers as if she'd been living in Japan all her life, and put them in a neat pair side by side, with the toes facing outward toward the street, because that was the way she would later exit. Underneath she wore white socks, the soles of which were pristine, like newly fallen snow. Growing up, we too had removed our shoes at the threshold of our door. I still remembered the shock of going over to a friend's house after school one day and being allowed to run around the garden barefoot. Her mother had turned on the sprinklers and at first the ground had hurt, but then it became soft and wet, the grass actually warm from the sun.

I put on a pair of slippers and went up to the ticket counter to pay. The woman there took my notes and handed back some coins for change, as well as two tickets and two pamphlets printed on beautiful white paper. She explained that there were two exhibitions on: some works from China and the Korean peninsula downstairs, and fabric and textiles from a famous artist upstairs. I thanked her and took the pamphlets, and turned around to relay this excitedly to my mother, thinking of her careful dress and how she had always perfectly repaired and adjusted all of our clothing when we were young. I suggested that we go around the exhibits separately, so that we could take as much time as we wanted, or not, with certain works. But I said, we would always be aware of each other and never too far away. I was worried that she would still want to be close to me, given her earlier fear at the station, but she seemed calmed by the space and its easy confines, and dutifully went into the next room with the pamphlet open in her hands as if she were about to read it.

The museum was spread across two levels. It was cool and quiet, with uneven wooden floors and large dark beams, and you could still see the old house that the building had once been. The stairs were low and small, because people had once been low and small, and they creaked and were bowed in the middle where many thousands of feet had shined them smooth. Through the windows came a soft, milky light, as through a paper screen. I chose a room at random, folding the pamphlet in half and putting it in my coat pocket. I wanted, somehow, to come to the works naively, to know little about their origin or provenance, to see them only as they were. Various pots and vases were displayed in glass cabinets, with handwritten cards that listed the era in which they were made, and a few other characters that I could not read. Each was somehow roughly formed but spirited. In their irregular shapes, both delicate and thick, it was possible to see that each had been made by hand, and had then been glazed and painted, also by hand, so that once, something as simple as a bowl from which you ate or a vessel from which you drank had been undifferentiated from art. I moved from room to room, taking a photo of a blue plate, the color of agate, on which white flowers, probably lotuses, were painted, and another of a mud-brown bowl, whose inside was the color of eggshells. For a while, I had been aware of my mother behind me, pausing where I paused, or moving quickly along when I did. But soon, I lost sight of her. I waited briefly in the last room on the ground floor to see if she might reappear, and then headed upstairs. On the way, I noticed that there was a room where a screen had been pushed back, and which overlooked a peaceful garden with stones and maple trees, the leaves of which were turning red.

The fabrics were hanging in a long room, such that you could look at all of them at once or each on its own. Some were small but some were so large that their tails draped and ran over the floor like frozen water and it was impossible to imagine them being worn or hanging in any room but this one. Their patterns were at once primitive and graceful, and as beautiful as the garments in a folktale. Looking at the translucency of the overlapping dyes reminded me of looking upward through a canopy of leaves. They reminded me of the seasons and, in their bare, visible threads, of something lovely and honest that had now been forgotten, a thing we could only look at but no longer live. I felt at the same time mesmerized by their beauty and saddened at this vague thought. I walked along the pieces many times and waited in the room for my mother. When she did not appear I went and explored the rest of the house alone and, in the end, found her waiting for me outside, sitting on the stone bench next to the stand where I had clipped our umbrellas.

I asked her if she had seen the fabrics and she said that she had seen a little of them, but had become tired, so was waiting for me here.

I wanted for some reason to speak more about the room, and what I had felt in it, that strange keenness. Wasn't it incredible, I wanted to say, that once there were people who were able to look at the world—leaves, trees, rivers, grass—and see its patterns, and, even more incredible, that they were able to find the essence of those patterns, and put them to cloth? But I found I could not. Instead I said that one of the rooms on the top floor, which looked down into the garden and across into the trees, had been designed for contemplation. You could slide open the window and sit at the narrow desk and watch the stones or the trees or the sky. Maybe it's good, I said, to stop sometimes and reflect upon the things that have happened, maybe thinking about sadness can actually end up making you happy.

That night, we went to a restaurant, in a tiny little street near the railway lines. I took us by a route along the canal, which I thought might be nice at that time of evening. The buildings around us were dark and the trees dark and quiet. Plants grew on the steep walls of the canal, trailing downward, and the water gave a shaking, delicate impression of the world above. Along the street, the restaurants and cafés had turned on only low, dim lights, like lanterns. Though we were in the middle of the city, it was like being in a village. This was one of the experiences I liked most about Japan, and, like so many things, it was halfway between a cliché and the truth. It's beautiful, I said, and my mother smiled but it was impossible to tell if she agreed.

The restaurant was on the top floor of a two-story building, and the stairs were so steep and narrow, going up them was almost like climbing a ladder. We were shown to a seat at a wooden counter, next to a narrow window overlooking the street, where, I noticed, it had again begun to rain. Because my mother did not eat living things, we ordered carefully. I read what I could from the menu, but needed her help more often than not with characters I did not understand or had forgotten and together we managed to find the right dishes. I could sense that she was relieved, finally, to be able to offer some help.

My mother looked out the window and said that it was raining again. I looked too, as if noticing for the first time, and said that yes it was. She said that even though it was October, she was not cold, that the climate here seemed milder, a light jacket was all she needed. She asked if it would rain tomorrow and I said I was not sure, but then I got out my phone to check and said that tomorrow looked clear, though I'd have to check again once we got back to the hotel. She said that she had felt strange the week before and had been worried that she would be ill for the trip, but she had rested and eaten well, and now she felt fine, and not even that tired. I asked her what she had thought of today, and she said that it had been very nice. Then she reached for her bag and took out a small book. She explained that she had found it at a store near her home, and that it described the nature of your character based on the day of your birth. She flipped to the right month and read out mine.

People born on your birthday, she said, are idealistic in their youth. In order to be truly free, they need to realize the impossibility of their dreams, and thus be humbled, and only then will they be happy. They like peace, order and beautiful things, but they can live entirely in their own heads.

She read out her own sign, and then the one for my sister, who she said was loyal and a hard worker, but was also quick to anger, and could hold a grudge for a very long time. Then she read out the part that told you who was most compatible with whom, comparing first of all her children to each other, and then each of them to herself.

I thought that some of it was true and some of it was not, but the real truth was how such things allowed someone to talk about you, or what you had done or why you did it, in a way that unraveled your character into distinct traits. It made you seem readable to them, or to yourself, which could feel like a revelation. But who's to say how anyone would act on a given day, not to mention the secret places of the soul, where all manner of things could exist? I wanted to talk more about this, if only to chase the thought further, to pin it down for myself, but I knew too that she needed, and wanted, to believe in such things: that my sister was generous and happiest in the company of others, that I should be careful with money in the month of May, so I said nothing.

The food arrived on two trays, with a bowl of white rice near the center, and various smaller plates of vegetables and garnishes on either side from which you could pick and choose many different flavors and textures. My mother commented a little on each one, seeming pleased with our combined effort. The way she used her chopsticks to move things from one plate to another, holding them with her fingers so that the ends never crossed, had always looked so elegant to me. I held my chopsticks the wrong way, jabbing and crossing them, and whenever I tried to emulate her style, I could not, and always ended up dropping things.

While we ate, I asked her again if there was anything in particular she wanted to see while we were here, any special garden or temple or landmark. She waved her hand in the air and said anything would do. She said that she had looked at a travel guide before coming here, but had decided not to buy it. Though on the cover, there was a photo of some bright red gates. I said that those were in Kyoto, and that if she was interested we could see them, as we would be finishing our trip there.

I finished eating first and put my chopsticks across the rim of my bowl and waited. Outside, the train tracks were dark and silent, splitting the road like a river. Men and women were cycling home, steering with one hand and holding up clear umbrellas with the other. Occasionally, someone would stop to buy something at the convenience store on the opposite side of the street, the windows of which were brightly lit and piled with brands whose colorful packaging I was beginning to recognize. I thought about how vaguely familiar this scene was to me, especially with the smells of the restaurant around me, but strangely so, because it was not my childhood, but my mother's childhood that I was thinking of, and from another country at that. And yet there was something about the subtropical feel, the smell of the steam and the tea and the rain. It reminded me of her photographs, or the television dramas we had watched together when I was still young. Or it was like the sweets she used to buy for me, which no doubt were the sweets her mother used to buy for her. It was strange at once to be so familiar and yet so separated. I wondered how I could feel so at home in a place that was not mine.

My mother pushed her bowl away and apologized, saying that she was unable to finish her food. I said it was fine and scooped the rest of her rice into mine, though I was not hungry. At the bottom of our bowls, which were ceramic, there was a small circle where the glaze had pooled and dried. It looked like liquid, like a blue pond, but when you tilted the bowl to the side, it never moved.

I had chosen a hotel in one of the city's busiest districts, with the station on one side and a view of a famous park on the other. At the time, I had been thinking not only of convenience, but of comfort, even luxury. Though now I wasn't so sure about my choice. The hotel was like any other, somehow always transitory, with the same heavy furniture that you would find in hotels all around the world. In this way, it was meant to provide comfort only because nothing should stand out or threaten. The corridors looked so similar I kept on turning the wrong way to get to our room, disoriented. While my mother had a shower, I sat on one of the twin beds and called my sister. There was a large window at one end of the room with a wide, cold ledge and heavy silked curtains, as well as a thinner, inner layer of gauze for when you wanted to see, or partially see, the shimmering outside. I pulled both of these back while I spoke on the phone, looking out to the red pilot lights that gleamed at the top of the skyscrapers and a tall structure that I thought might be Tokyo Tower.

My sister picked up and we said hello and I asked her for her news. She said that her daughter had been wearing the same dress for three days straight. She took it off only to bathe, but then even slept in it. She said that before our mother had left for Japan, she had been looking after the children one morning at a department store while my sister ran some errands. There, her daughter had insisted on buying the dress, and when our mother had expressed reluctance, had thrown her first ever public tantrum. Panicking, our mother had relented and paid. The dress, my sister said, was both ugly and expensive, but her daughter had seen something in it, something that connected to a feeling deep inside her, that she was not yet old enough to express. It was also too short, and my sister had had to sew on a layer of leftover lace around the hem, even though she knew her daughter would grow out of that too very quickly. Now, both her children were playing out in the garden, and each day, the dress, which was a pale wheat color, became dirtier and dirtier.

My sister too had been prone to deep rages as a child. I mentioned this and she said yes, she remembered, though she had barely thought of this until her daughter's own episode. I remembered her smashing a glass wand against the brick wall of our house once. The wand had been filled with glitter and water, so that the contents tumbled magically from one end to the other depending on how you tilted it. The object had been precious to us both and now neither of us could remember why she had broken it, only our devastation once the act had been done. I asked my sister if she could remember the source of her anger back then and she said no, not really. She said that over the years, her anger had faded, and now, oddly, she had a reputation for being calm and levelheaded, especially at her work, where she was often praised for her competence. But, witnessing her daughter, it was like remembering the details of a dream she once had, that perhaps, at some point in her life, there had been things worth screaming and crying over, some deeper truth, or even horror, that everyone around you perpetually denied, which only made you angrier and angrier. Yet now, my sister could not harness that feeling, only the memory of it, or not even that, but something even more remote. All that was left for her to do, she said, was to allow her daughter to wear the same dress for days on end, to sew on a new hem, to make her something warm for dinner, to look on her in flawed understanding, and console in all the insufficient ways.

She asked how the trip was going, sounding tired. I knew she was also studying for her last round of medical exams, the ones that would help her specialize, involving a knowledge and technicality that I could not even imagine. I said I wasn't sure. I couldn't quite tell if our mother was here because she wanted to be, or if it was something she was doing for my sake.

At dinner, my mother had asked about my own life. I had said that Laurie and I were wondering about whether or not to have children. My mother said that we should, that children were a good thing. At the time, I had agreed. But what I really wanted to say was that we talked about it often, while cooking dinner or walking to the shops or making coffee. We talked about every aspect over and over, each of us adding tiny lifelike details, or going over hundreds of different possibilities, like physicists in endless conjecture. How hurtful would we be when we were both exhausted and sleep-deprived? Would there be enough money? How would we stay fulfilled while at the same time caring so completely for another? We asked our friends, all of whom were frank and honest. Some of them said that it was possible to find a way, especially as their children got older. Others said that all the weakest points of our relationship would be laid bare. Others still said that it was a euphoric experience, if only you surrendered yourself to it. And yet really, these thoughtful offerings meant nothing, because it was impossible, ultimately, to compare one life to another, and we always ended up essentially in the same place where we had begun. I wondered if my mother had ever asked these questions, if she'd ever had the luxury of them. I had never particularly wanted children, but somehow I felt the possibility of it now, as lovely and elusive as a poem. Another part of me wondered if it was okay either way, not to know, not be sure. That I could let life happen to me in a sense, and that perhaps this was the deeper truth all along, that we controlled nothing and no one, though really I didn't know that either.

My mother had said that she wanted to buy something for my sister's children, and so the next day we went to a large department store where she spent some time carefully browsing through the aisles. In the children's section, she lingered between a gray shirt and a blue one, between a large backpack and a small. She held each one up to me as if I were a mirror and asked what I thought. I said I liked the blue shirt and the large backpack, even though I knew that, in reality, it would be impossible to predict what my sister's children would like, since their favorite things and possessions changed constantly and unpredictably, as if driven by other laws, of which we had no understanding. What was precious and completely necessary one week was discarded the next, and equally, what had been neglected suddenly became a favorite again. At the counter, the sales assistant wrapped the gifts beautifully, with tissue paper the color of candy and boxes and thin, delicate ribbons. I could tell my mother was pleased, even though I suspected my niece and nephew would not have the patience to cope with these layers anyway, and would probably rip them apart.

The night before, we had walked back to the station along the little streets that followed the curve of the railway line. The pavement had been dark, the night dense, as under the canopy of a forest, but along the way there were a few shops still open, their light glowing like the light from a small house in a valley, seen from a distance. Bicycles were left standing outside, and, from some wooden awnings, one or two red paper lanterns hung. I said to my mother there was a good bookshop along the way, that I knew was open late, and that I wanted to stop at. I had been there before with Laurie. His father was a sculptor and it was mostly through Laurie that I had first learned about art, though, comparatively, I still knew very little. Visiting the shop for the first time, we had been amazed to find such a beautiful collection of secondhand art books, in both English and Japanese.

I recognized the building and pushed open the door to the sound of a tiny bell. Inside, it was as calm and quiet as a library. Some piano music was playing, and, after a while, I recognized a few bars. It was the same song I had heard as a student when walking through the university's music school one evening, during one of those particular solitary, slightly abstract moments when a fragment of music can seem especially beautiful. A milky light had been placed on the countertop, its glow giving the impression of a large candle. I wandered about the shelves, looking at the titles. Among a section on painters at the back, I found a large hardback on landscapes, with a chapter on a series of paintings that I remembered seeing when I was still studying. At the time, I thought that the paintings were sketches, done somehow with watercolors or chalks. This was because they had given only the vaguest impression of mountains and beaches, roads and cliffs and lakes, in such a way that everything seemed formless, or ghostlike, lifted perhaps from a memory or a dream. It was as if the artist had smeared them onto the paper with only his fingers, or as if the paintings had been submerged soon after being completed, leaving only clouded patches of color and ink. It was only much later that I learned that the artist was much more widely known for his other paintings—of dancers, or women in baths. I learned too that the landscapes were not done only with paint, but via a kind of printing with oils and plates and paper, finished sometimes with pastels, and it was these second or third impressions that gave them their forgotten quality, like things glimpsed and remembered from the window of a speeding train. I called my mother over to show her, and to explain to her the method of their creation, so that she would not make the same mistake as I had. I found other books and showed her a few other works that I admired and thought she might like, sculptures and carvings that aimed to capture the essence of life, birth, hope or despair. For each one, I explained their context, their intent, and a little about the circumstances in which they had been made. I asked her if she would like me to buy her something from the shop. She said that there was no need, that she did not know what to choose. I told her it could be anything, all she had to do was pick what she was most drawn to, but she seemed hesitant to even reach for a book, pointing instead at one, seemingly at random, and saying this one, her voice like a question. Eventually I ended up choosing for her, a slim volume of art history from an English writer. The woman at the counter was about my age, and while putting through the sale, she asked me a few questions about my choice and then about myself. I explained where we were from, and that I was traveling with my mother around Japan. We spoke a little about the artist, and she told me that she had studied in London, and while there had traveled to Morocco and Bhutan. She wished us well and gave me the book in a paper bag tied with red string, which I took and handed to my mother.

After leaving the department store, we caught a train to one of the city's central business districts, to a gallery located on the fifty-third floor of a fifty-four-story tower. The building had been constructed on a wide hill and its exterior, blue-green and reflective, had reportedly been designed to resemble samurai armor. At the top, there was a view of all of Tokyo. The walls were steel and glass, and beyond us the city beamed outward: low-lying and moonlike and, in certain mauvish lights, chalk-white. Once inside the gallery, we were led to a short queue and told to remove our shoes and wait. Every twenty minutes or so, groups of ten or twelve were admitted into what looked like a dark and silent room. An attendant came round and showed us a line drawing of the room on a clipboard and explained that inside it would be completely dark, but that we would be able to feel our way by running our hands along the walls. Then, we would come to some benches, where we could sit. When our turn came, we did as she had instructed. I could see nothing at all, not a thing in front of me, not even an outline. Somehow, the enveloping blackness of the room made us all silent too, in a way that was both anticipatory and slightly unbearable. I thought of my sister, probably at work right now on her rounds. Beside me, two French tourists burst out laughing, unable to take it any longer. And then a small square of orange light began to appear in the distance. It was as faint as the dawn and, like the dawn, we had to wait a long time until we could fully see it. Eventually, it became bigger, and brighter, but so slowly that it was impossible to be aware of these changes. Yet equally, because it was the only visible thing in the room, we could not help but stare at the light with intense focus. After a long while, we were told that we could stand up and approach. I walked forward slowly. My eyes were still adjusting and the room now seemed to be a deep, impenetrable blue, like the blue of an evening, and it was suddenly hard to trust what I saw in front of me. The ground seemed to be at the same level as my face. Getting closer, I saw that the light came not from a screen, as I had thought, but from a square-shaped hollow perfectly cut into the wall, another thing I had failed to notice.

In the gallery's café, we found a table for two by the window and I ordered two "image cakes," inspired by the exhibition, and two green teas. While we ate, I asked my mother what she had thought of the work we had just seen and she looked up at me in a brief panic, as if called to give an answer to a question she did not understand. I said that it was all right, that she should feel free to answer truthfully, with whatever she thought. I said that if she still had the energy, there was one more gallery that I would like us to see, not far, but just a few stations away. Actually, the gallery was a bit further than I let on. I could see that she was tired. All I had to do was to tell her not to worry about it, that we had seen enough today, and could go back to the hotel to rest. But for some reason, I let the question hang in the air, and doing so was like applying a kind of firm but gentle pressure. After a moment she nodded and I nodded too and collected our plates.

The exhibition was a collection of some works by Monet and several other impressionist painters. The building was cramped and badly lit, and many of the works hung in fussy, elaborate frames. But each still contained a world unto itself, of cities and ports, of mornings and evenings, of trees and paths and gardens and ever-changing light. Each showed the world not as it was but some version of the world as it could be, suggestions and dreams, which were, like always, better than reality and thus unendingly fascinating. I stood with my mother in front of one of the main paintings of the exhibition and said that actually, I thought I understood.

Earlier, she had asked about a book I was reading, and I explained that it was a modern retelling of a Greek myth. I said that for a long time, I had loved these stories. In part, it was because they had an eternal metaphoric quality that you could use to speak for almost anything in life: love, death, beauty, grief, fate, wars, violence, family, oaths, funerals. I said it was almost like how painters had once used the camera obscura: by looking indirectly at the thing they wanted to focus on, they were sometimes able to see it even more clearly than with their own eyes. I said that I had spent a year of my university degree studying these texts. In one of my first classes, we had pushed back the desks and put our chairs in a rough semicircle and listened as the lecturer spoke about the Trojan War. I said that compared to the strictness of the Catholic school we had gone to, the one she had striven so hard for us to attend, where you could not so much as have one button on your shirt undone or your hair shorter than your chin, this gesture in itself seemed revolutionary. For the rest of the semester, the lecturer spoke about the Greeks, how some of their greatest plays actually spoke of their own guilt as a slave-owning society, in which women were also kept mute, and most of all about their guilt about what they had done to Troy. Such was their remorse, that they took this incident, which could have vanished into history, and made with it some of their most lasting and tragic art. She said that then, almost like now, much of their literature and governance was based on the sacred rules of hospitality. First, the Trojans had violated this rule by taking Helen, and then the Greeks themselves had repaid the favor with their deadly gift of the wooden horse, as well as all the other violations that take place throughout their stories. She said that these feelings were still very much alive in us today. Then she had spoken of her own childhood, in which her mother had somehow kept an unspoken tally of all giving and receiving, not only among friends but also within the family. She remembered the perfect gifts that her mother had taken with them whenever they visited other houses, a formality that, as an adolescent, she had often found excruciating, and how her mother always remarked upon anything that had been given to her in turn, weighing it up like justice upon invisible scales. Throughout her childhood, they had lived in a big house and had had many guests and relatives stay, yet nothing was done without this tally, which no one ever spoke about, and as an adult, she had to work very hard to eradicate the similar calculations going on in her own mind.

That year, I was hungry for everything this lecturer said, for every book and play mentioned in her class. I was fascinated with how the characters spoke in great figurative monologues, giving full voice to their rage and grief with a precision that would have been impossible in any real speech. I was shocked, also, to learn that several of my classmates had already read these texts, and were familiar with their theories and interpretations. To them, the lecturer was not revelatory, but simply repeating ideas that were already very old. Not only that, they seemed to know many other things as well: films and books and plays and artists, whose names they dropped into conversation with an ease that signaled something. When a girl in my class spoke of a particular film in relation to Antigone, she did so smoothly and naturally, her eyes flicking across the room as if to see who else recognized this name. When her eyes went to me, I immediately looked down. How did they know all these people, all these works? How had they managed to read and watch so much in only the first few weeks of the semester? The girl knew so much without seeming to try, and she seemed complete, defined in some way that I wasn't.

The lecturer had spoken about knowledge as an elixir and I said to my mother that this was something I believed in too. In the Catholic school, my sister and I had both studied very hard. If there was anything I did not know, I simply read and reread everything I could until nothing about it was a mystery to me any longer. In this way, I was like the runner in a marathon, made up only of will and perseverance. In school, I had done this repeatedly, and it had worked. There, I had understood everything, and passed all my subjects with the highest marks. During that class, I tried to do the same. I read all the plays, and then the books on the plays, and then the books on those. I watched films and read about artists and directors and poets. Each time, it was like I was traveling at the speed of light, as if I had spent all my life living in one dimension, only for its very fabric to tear open and a whole other universe to be revealed. Every time I finished a text, I felt like I was done, but then the same thing would happen again and again, a tearing open of my thoughts, a falling into a vast, unknown space, where the air rushed and all my senses were overwhelmed. It was as if this knowledge was truly an elixir, a drug. And yet, something eluded me. By the end of the year, I had written many words on these texts, and now knew them as well as anyone else. I too mentioned them in conversation, I too could be confident, and my thoughts felt rapid and full. But all the same, I felt that there was something else, something fundamental, that I did not understand.

At the end of the year, the lecturer said that she would be holding a party at her house for some of her colleagues and other students. She said that her children would be there, and that we were all invited too. I had become fascinated with the lecturer, with the way she spoke, her knowledge, her gestures. She seemed to have no boundary between the academic and the personal, and regularly told us things in class that I, with my Catholic schooling, found both shocking and riveting. One day she came in and declared that her father's house had been flooded over the weekend in a terrible storm. Everything was gone, she said. They had waded through the wreckage to find whatever they could—books, heirlooms, photo albums. She had taken her father and his partner in like they were refugees, gathering clothes and bedding from friends. The loss was evident on her face. She made no attempt to hide her grief, which must have been her father's grief also, and this surprised me, that she would not try and mask it somehow, that she was not ashamed of the drama, as my family would have been, but inhabited it with rage and sadness, as if it were the cloak of some great animal that she had just slain. I wanted badly to please her, to win her approval. I studied hard, and when I wrote my essays, I wrote them not just for a good mark, but tried to add extra depth and inflection with her in mind. At the same time, I was worried that my earnestness was overdone, and that far from impressing her, it would lead her to dislike me, so at the same time, I kept a calm, restrained facade, which I realized seemed to suit me as well.

I did not know if anyone else would show up to the lecturer's party. I dragged my sister to the shops in our neighborhood, trying to find something to wear. I knew by then that you did not wear dresses to this sort of thing, or at least the kind of dresses I might have once worn to parties. Rather, the special trick lay in wearing something that was both casual and instinctive, and that looked striking but essentially unplanned. Eventually, I settled on blue jeans and a bright-red knitted T-shirt. I wore my hair up in a loose knot and brought with me a bottle of wine from the shop down the road.

The lecturer lived in a suburb near the university. The house was bigger than I had expected and was surrounded by a high concrete wall, covered in ivy. Behind it there was a large and beautiful garden, with paths made from old brick pavers and three olive trees. In the middle of the garden, there was a big, heavy wooden table, piled with food and drink, just like the banquets and feasts we had studied and read about in the plays that year. A dog, beautiful and reddish, ran around happily, tumbling over the green, well-watered grass. I stood for a while, looking, breathing in something strong and fragrant, and realized that I was standing in a small orchard of fruit trees, upon which paper lanterns had been hung. Eventually I found the lecturer and gave her the wine and she kissed me on both cheeks. Looking at the other bottles on the table, I realized that the wine I had brought was wrong, that instead of something that suited this setting, I had chosen something ridiculous and sweet and childlike. But the lecturer didn't seem to mind. I noticed she was wearing a pair of incredibly beautiful earrings, long and multicolored, which framed her face like a headdress. I could not help but tell her so and she smiled and pointed over to where some others from my class were sitting. I was relieved to see them and slipped quickly into their circle, saying, in my excitement, that this looked and felt exactly like a scene from a film that we had all talked about. Back then, I had wanted every moment to count for something; I had become addicted to the tearing of my thoughts, that rent in the fabric of the atmosphere. If nothing seemed to be working toward this effect, I grew impatient, bored. Much later, I realized how insufferable this was: the need to make every moment pointed, to read meaning into everything. Yet every single one of my classmates back then seemed to be the same. Conversation was like a kind of judo, an exercise in constant movement. I felt a small sense of triumph when I was able to talk with them about the right kinds of books and films. And when I was able to say something unique about them, it was like I had won something, a tiny victory. We talked as if we were dancing, and danced until we were delirious. It was all so beautiful, I kept thinking, and perhaps saying out loud too. I could not seem to believe that this world existed, and that I had somehow got entrance to it.

Toward the end of the night, I walked around the garden and into the house. There were empty wine glasses on the big table, and scrunched up paper napkins stained purple on the ground. The dog was resting in the corner with its head on its paws. In the orchard, apple cores were scattered on the ground, some newly bitten, some probably from days or weeks before. Inside, the music had stopped playing but there was still the noise of gentle chatter from the garden. I gathered up the wine glasses as I went, tipping the excess out onto the ground. I had worked for years at a restaurant and I knew how to clear a big table. I piled up the plates on top of each other, carrying the cutlery and napkins on the top, and the wine glasses upside down by their stems between my fingers. In the kitchen, I tipped the scraps of food into the trash and stacked the empty wine bottles in a neat row. Then I filled the sink up with hot water and soap, and carefully washed the glasses and plates. Soon, the water was dark and cloudy. The heat made the room smell of old wine, fragrant and thick. I drained the sink and filled it again with clean water and more soap, and washed whatever was left. When I was done, I stacked the plates neatly on the dish rack to dry. Then I found a clean tea towel and dried the glasses until they were clear and unmarked, and left them in neat rows on the bench top. I wiped everything down and wrung out the cloth. And then I got my bag, and left.

The next day, the lecturer emailed to thank me for helping to clean up, though she said I did not have to do it. She also said that she would be going away for a few weeks over the summer, and asked if I would like to look after the house and the dog. I could not believe how lucky I was, to get to visit that house again, but this time on my own. When the time came, I packed some clean clothes in a bag, and got the key that the lecturer had given me the week before out of its yellow envelope. As I walked up the same street, the house seemed even bigger than it had before. I unlocked the gate and pushed against it, disturbing the ivy vines that were growing over the inside wall. The dog bounded up to me and I let it sniff my hand for a few moments before bending down to stroke its lovely, flat head. When I reached for the soft, warm spots behind its ears, it half closed its eyes, as if lightly hypnotized. I left my bag by the door and went from room to room, taking everything in. In the daylight I could see how high the ceilings were, how the light streamed through certain windows and hit the walls, like the bare alcoves of a contemporary museum.

A large, generous fruit bowl rested on the kitchen countertop, looking as if it was simply waiting to be filled with plums or apples or bunches of grapes. There were recipe books in the cabinets and clean, modern-looking utensils which I had never seen before, things like a pasta press, a mortar and pestle, or a shallow but heavy pan with a curled handle at either end. Many of the walls contained floor-to-ceiling bookshelves, and these were filled with books. Some of the authors I had heard of and not yet read, but there were also many I had never even heard of before. There was an entire section on Greek literature, and another in French, and I realized that the lecturer must be fluent in both these languages in order to read in them. I thought what a shame it was I was only staying two weeks; I would have been able to spend months reading my way through all these books, and perhaps then I would be closer to whatever quality it was my lecturer, or the girl in my class, seemed to have.

Over the next few days, I was both the guest and the host. I walked the dog along the paths by the river and through the park, letting it lead me wherever it wanted, waiting until it had sniffed and explored to its heart's content. I looked through the recipe books in the generous kitchen and bookmarked the ones I wanted to try, writing the ingredients down carefully on a piece of paper. Then, sometime during the next day, I would go to the nearby market, wheeling a trolley I had found in the house that seemed like a better version of the ones often seen in the cheap discount stores near where we lived, the kind that sold floor mats or mops or colored buckets in bulk. I cooked something new each evening, carefully following the instructions, as if they were for a detailed experiment in a lab, enjoying the weight of the heavy pans and stirrers, the way the exhaust fan, which was so silent I sometimes thought I had not switched it on, sucked up the steam from boiling water so completely it was like magic. There were many different bowls in the cupboards and many different types of cutlery, but for some reason, I always chose the same ones and sat on the same stool at the end of the kitchen counter, rather than at the big dining table or the smaller table near the conservatory, as if keen to make my presence in the house as light as possible. Sometimes, I poured myself a glass of wine and dimmed the lights, or else played a record, turning the volume up so that the music filled the whole house. If it was warm, I opened the windows and on those nights the scent of the lilacs that grew near the fence would drift in from the garden, blending with the music and with my solitary meal.

Keeping in mind, too, the role of the guest, I was careful not to look in any closets or open anything that looked private. But I let my eyes roam freely about the surfaces of the house itself, which was full of objects and paintings that the lecturer had brought back from her travels. In this way, the house was like a museum, and, as I looked through everything, I had a feeling that all of this was very carefully chosen, that every object spoke in some way about the lecturer, or her family, about the choices they had made, and what they felt to be the purpose of their lives, though I could not have said exactly how.

The lecturer had said that I was welcome to have people over and so during the middle of the stay, I asked my sister and some of my classmates to come. I cooked several dishes that I had already made from the cookbooks, and brought these out to the big wooden table in the garden. During the lunch—perhaps because the day was beautiful and the orchard peaceful, and perhaps also because we were all young, drinking and talking and laughing, and because I had tied my hair back with a scarf as blue as the cobalt of Delft tableware—I had again the sensation of seeing us like a still in a film, or a photograph, and the feeling was paired with another one of satisfaction, and rightness. In the kitchen, I found several small blue and white bowls, much like the ones that we had in our house, with a decorative border around the rim and what looked like translucent grains of rice arranged in a flowerlike pattern around the sides. I used these to serve the sweet-savory

Cantonese dessert I had made, which was a recipe of my mother's, the only one of hers that I had cooked during my stay.

It was generous and warm living there, and I felt more and more at home each day. On the last night, I filled the large bathtub with almost scalding hot water and dropped into it a few beads of amber-colored oil. I lay in the tub, with the dog resting on the floor nearby, until the water began to cool, at which point I turned the hot water tap with my foot until the temperature rose back up. I did this for almost two hours, until the water reached almost to the brim, threatening to spill over, before reluctantly pulling the plug and getting out.

Afterward, I sent the lecturer an email, thanking her for allowing me to stay and saying that everything had been pleasant and easy. What I did not write about was the fact that, as pleasant as it had been, something continued to elude me, both in the house and afterward, a feeling I could not quite shake. When I returned home, I was, for a time, confused. I picked my normal routine back up: I enrolled in a summer course, reading more books, writing more essays, and wandered around the near-empty campus, where only a handful of students and lecturers remained. When the restaurant reopened after its short break, I went back to my job as a waitress, leaving in the evening and returning late at night, eating a supper of plain rice with whatever leftovers the kitchen had given us around midnight, before falling into bed. Sometimes, I went with my sister or my mother to the market, and together we cooked the dishes we had cooked all our lives. While eating, we did not discuss the Greeks or languages or films the way my classmates had at the lecturer's house, but rather the meal and the food, from the freshness of the ingredients to the cheapness of their cost. I did not mention the different things I had experimented with at the lecturer's house, how I had sat, in almost decadent solitude, with my single glass of wine each night, thinking over the day. Somehow, it felt like I was living my life from the outside in. I picked up objects that had long been mine—clothes, makeup, books—and at times it was as if they did not belong to me but were a stranger's. I looked at the white pot with the tiny feet, out of which a bonsai had once grown, and for a brief moment despised it. I looked at the little blue and white bowls in our kitchen. We ate regularly out of these bowls. They were exactly the same as the ones in the lecturer's house, and yet also entirely different. I realized that part of the problem was that I was seeing these things, noting them, when before I would not have given them a second glance, though I still could not work out why or to what end. And then one day I had a thought. I realized that the lecturer's house was really like a museum, or like certain lessons of history: a smooth and fluid line. Our house, in contrast, was like a postmodern array, a jumble of colors and noise and objects that, for a long time, I had to struggle to silence, and to forget, and of which I could not help but feel vaguely ashamed. I couldn't put it any other way. Nothing much changed after that, except that for a long while, I also stopped reading the Greeks. By the time I returned to them, much later, I was almost disappointed to find that I was enthralled by them still.

By then, I had also learned about the history of the blue and white porcelain, which had existed in some form or another in both the lecturer's house and mine. I had been flipping through a book on East Asian art at someone's house, a friend of a friend, whom I did not know well, when I had come across an image of two vases that were also blue and white. Everyone else was talking in the kitchen, but I had stopped turning the pages and bent over the image. I recognized the pattern immediately, only there was a clear difference with these vases: the shapes were somehow finer, with smooth shoulders and elegant lines, the white milkier, and the blue lighter and faded, as if applied with a brush. I read there about how the porcelain had been made for hundreds of years in China, and how it was traded not only as far as Europe but also the Middle East, appearing in the paintings of Rembrandt van Rijn, or as tablets inscribed with verses from the Quran. I read about how, for a long time, porcelain was much prized, in part because the secret to its composition was still a mystery. The wares were exported to Europe and some came to feature Dutch houses or Christian iconography alongside lotus petals and traditional *ruyi* borders. These, made specially to order, were named Chine de commande. Later, the secret to porcelain making was discovered in Germany and England, and Chinese porcelain became less singular and less needed.

I turned to my mother, who was still looking at the Monet, which happened to be one of his most famous pieces. She was swaying lightly on her feet, as if to music, or as if very tired. I said that I too sometimes did not understand what I saw in galleries, or read in books. Though I understood the pressure of feeling like you had to have a view or opinion, especially one that you could articulate clearly, which usually only came with a certain education. This, I said, allowed you to speak of history and context, and was in many ways like a foreign language. For a long time, I had believed in this language, and I had done my best to become fluent in it. But I said that sometimes, increasingly often in fact, I was beginning to feel like this kind of response too was false, a performance, and not the one I had been looking for. Sometimes, I looked at a painting, and felt completely nothing. Or if I had a feeling, it was only intuitive, a reaction, nothing that could be expressed in words. It was all right, I said, to simply say if that was so. The main thing was to be open, to listen, to know when and when not to speak.

We walked through the cemetery at Aoyama. The famous cherry trees were bare, and all around us the vertical stones gave the impression of little shrines. They seemed less like graves than houses and plots for tiny spirits, and indeed some were surrounded by what might be called gates or wooden fences, while others featured miniature stone lanterns, or stone vases, where flowers had been placed. Stone, moss, swept leaves, writing on wooden posts. I was reminded for some reason of a forest or monastery. Earlier, we had gone to a large outdoor museum in Koganei Park, where old Japanese houses had been transported and rebuilt, to give an idea of what life was like during the Edo period. Inside one, a woman invited us to sit and served us hot tea from a pot over an open fire. The taste was flowery, but not exactly sweet. I looked into the cup and saw a pink blossom. The woman said the tea was made from sakura petals, which had been preserved in salt. Looking around the house, with its bare dirt floors and firewood stove, my mother said that it reminded her of her childhood home. How could it, though, when this house was over two hundred years old? But I knew that she meant the bare floor, the simple kitchen with no electricity, the dimness. There were still streets like that in Hong Kong, remnants of tiny villages, crammed into the spaces between skyscrapers, or on rooftops, with electricity cables and washing lines strung between houses. She had told me once that as a girl she had seen a man jump from a five-story balcony, and another time a dog being beaten by the roadside.

It occurred to me that by the age I was now, my mother had already made a new life for herself in a new country. She would have, by then, already become mother to a new baby, and would likely have been able to count the number of times that she would return to Hong Kong to see her family on one hand. I tried, and failed, to imagine her first months there. Had she been homesick? Had she been awed by the streets, the brick and weatherboard houses, so different from her own home? Had she been worn out not by the big changes, but, as is often the case, by countless smaller ones—the supermarkets that were so well stocked, but where you could not buy glass noodles, or the right kind of rice; the homes where porridge was something plain and tasteless, made with oats and milk instead of with thinly sliced scallions, bamboo shoots, and black, hundred-year eggs; the roads where the people shouted at her from the cars when she crossed the street, for reasons she could not yet understand; the bank teller unable to understand her near-perfect, colonial English?

After drinking the tea, we wandered into an old communal bathhouse. The large room was separated by a low dividing wall, one half for women, the other for men. The baths were deep and square, covered in light blue tiles. Along the walls, there were a series of taps and mirrors, where, I explained, sitting on low stools, women would wash themselves first before entering the larger communal baths. Above, there was a large mural with blue skies, mountains, greenery, clouds and a large blue lake, as lovely and simple as an illustration in a children's picture book. My mother went up to look at it, craning her neck and sighing, as if it were not a painted wall but a view of a wide and pleasant vista. I took a photo of the mural, whose colors reminded me of the posters used to promote sporting events like the Olympics in the sixties and seventies, then of the blue tiles, and asked her if she would like to visit one of the bathhouses in Tokyo with me. I said I had been to one on my last trip and had enjoyed the experience, all the women and children bathing together. She said that she had not brought her bathing suit and I said that this didn't matter, in fact, swimsuits were not allowed. My mother smiled and shook her head. I thought of how, at the bathhouse, the babies and younger children had clung to their mothers as they bathed them, tipping water over their heads while holding up a hand to protect their eyes, how they did not feel truly separated from each other yet, but rather still part of the same body, the same spirit. There was, I knew, a time when my sister and I would have felt the same. On this trip, my mother was often dressed and ready before I was. If I happened to wake and see her getting out of bed in her pajamas, she would quickly go to the bathroom to change, even giving a little bow, in the Japanese way, before closing the door.

We had an early train to Ibaraki, and as we walked to the station wheeling our bags, the sky was dim and almost as dark as the room in the gallery had been the day before. Beneath our feet, the pavement seemed to glow slightly, and we passed by a few people on their way to work, wearing long brown coats with the collars turned up or holding slim briefcases. I told my mother that today we would travel for hours, taking a slight detour to see only one thing. I had been worried that we would miss our train, which would mean missing other connecting trains, and had rushed us out of the hotel. But we in fact arrived with more than enough time. I looked at the board and noticed that an even earlier train was due to arrive within minutes. I asked my mother to wait with our bags and went quickly to one of the ticket machines at the other end of the platform. I thought I remembered that it was somehow possible to change your tickets via one of these machines for an earlier service, but I was also aware that I might not make it in time. I knew my mother would be slightly worried to be separated during this moment of transit, that behind her calmness she would be willing me to hurry. I inserted our tickets and tried to navigate the menu, pressing the buttons for the English option, aware that the train would be arriving any minute. I moved quickly from screen to screen and eventually the machine took the tickets and, after a long pause, pushed out two new ones. I grabbed these and ran back toward my mother, who waved her hands as if to urge me excitedly on, just as the train was pulling into the platform.

Once we found our seats, my mother took my coat and hung it up on one of the little plastic hooks that you could flip out from the wall, while I pushed our bags up to the overhead rack. I asked her if she would like to have one of the books I had brought to read, or else the newspaper I had taken from the hotel that morning, but she shook her head and said she was happy to look at the view. She sat very straight, with her hands in her lap, and stared out the window to where the countryside was zipping by. The train was going so fast that the view was only a blur, an impression of colors and lines, such that it would have been impossible to take in any pleasurable detail. My mother commented that my uncle had liked trains, even though he had not been able to take them very often, and would have enjoyed this one.

I remembered that my mother had once told me a story about my uncle, whom I met on the few trips we had taken back to Hong Kong. He was quiet and slim, with the bookish air of the university student he had never been. Like my mother, he took care with his clothes and appearance, always wearing a white pressed shirt and black shoes, combing his hair to the side and with a slight wave, in the manner of Chinese film stars of the thirties and forties. My mother said that unlike most of the other boys in their neighborhood, my uncle was kind and thoughtful. He worked for a man at the bird market and would sometimes bring a few birds home with him. As a girl, my mother had loved having these in the house. Eight whole years separated them—in between my grandmother had had two miscarriages. My mother had often watched as her older brother cleaned the cages, and was sometimes allowed to help with the containers of water, which she filled in the kitchen sink and brought back to him, careful not to spill a drop, so that he could fit them back inside the cages, the floors of which he had already covered with fresh newspaper.

One day, a man came into the shop and spent a long time looking at the birds, asking my uncle to bring down this cage or that one from where they hung from long poles attached to the ceiling. My uncle was always careful to lower the cages smoothly, knowing that if the movement was too quick or uneven, the birds would grow distressed and attempt to fly around inside, which might lead to a damaged leg or wing. Eventually, the man selected two of the prettiest, most expensive birds, ones with heart-shaped chests and blush-colored feathers, saying that they were a present for his daughter. They are like a couple, he joked. My uncle made the sale, the last of the day, and closed up shop, shutting first the sliding wooden doors and locking them, and then the folding metal gates.

It was monsoon season, and often during those days my uncle would walk home in the rain, which at times was so fierce and sudden, you barely had time to open your umbrella before getting wet. No matter where you walked, your shoes would be soaked and the cuffs of your pant legs also. And then, just as quickly, the rain would clear, to be replaced with an equally thick and oppressive heat. On the day he was paid each month, my uncle would, upon coming home, take out the envelope and give two thirds to his mother, keeping only a little for himself.

One morning, my mother told me, my uncle had unlocked the wooden doors of the shop to find someone already waiting outside the metal gates. Through their pattern of chrysanthemums, he saw that it was a student, and recognized her uniform from the local convent school, the one very near his own, which he had left at fourteen to begin work. In her hands she held a shoebox, with six holes on the lid that had been made, it seemed, with a common lead pencil. When he opened the box, my uncle found one of the birds he had sold to the man a month before, weak and shivering, in a bed that had been made out of torn strips of old school socks. My uncle took one of the cages down and moved its bird in with another. Then he cleaned the cage thoroughly, adjusted the perch so that it was low and near to the floor, and added fresh newspaper, food and water. The girl left for school, and during the next few days he kept the cage near eye level while working at the shop, moving it into patches of dappled sunlight when it was warm, or else pulling the screen door partially closed to shield it when the rains came. Later, when the bird was finally able to fly up to the perch, which he had adjusted to sit higher and higher as the bird improved, he carried the cage, with a heavy cloth draped over the bamboo frame, to the girl's house, which was really more of a compound, on a well-known street.

In the days and weeks that followed, my mother said she would often catch glimpses of her brother and the girl together—riding their bikes across the city or waiting in line at a roadside stall. Sometimes, they invited her, taking her with them to the local sweet shop where they could fill a bag with dried plums and candy. She became accustomed to their usual meeting spots—at the fountain in the park, or the corner near the girl's convent school. It did not need to be said that the girl's parents would disapprove of them spending time together, because my uncle was poor and uneducated. More often than not, they made plans, and met, in secret. My mother in turn became an accomplice, her presence an easy cover for anyone who might see them, her youth, at ten, an unspoken chaperone. I had often wondered, hearing this, how my mother must have felt then. She would have been young enough for this to be her first real contact with romance, and old enough to be intrigued by it. Did she notice, for example, while perched on her brother's bike, or climbing the equipment in the playground, what it was like to have two people suddenly so concentrated on one another? How, even as they paid for her sweets, or bought her a ticket to the movies, their attention was rarely fully on the task at hand. How their jokes were meant to make only the other laugh, how happy they were? Did she watch all of this, I wondered, thinking, or dreaming, about what might lie ahead in her own future?

Her brother had always had an interest in cameras, and had bought one secondhand from what was left of his pay. He often took pictures when they were all out together, and because he was always the photographer, the only record of the relationship turned out to be photos of my mother and the girl together. She still had the photos somewhere, she said, a series taken at the fountain in the park, my mother standing up on its ledge, the girl sitting next to her in a long skirt, smiling, the water like a black and silver plate behind them. My mother said that at the time, she of course had felt that the girl was very sophisticated, almost an adult. She wore white school socks up to her ankles and carried her books bound together by a thick colored band. She was beautiful, with the pale complexion so valued in those days, and wore her hair in a ponytail, held together by a hair tie adorned with two white beads, the size of marbles. She had always been kind to my mother, whom she called little sister, and one day whispered in her ear about their plans to run away together once the school year was out.

But of course, despite their caution, everyone knew about the romance. The girl had told her friends at school, and my uncle's boss had seen her waiting outside the shop for him. Neighbors and friends spotted them riding their bikes together down toward the bay or sharing Western food at the local drinking house. It was an open secret.

One day, my uncle waited at their usual meeting spot near the school, but the girl did not come. He eventually went back to the school and found one of her classmates, who said that the girl had not been there that day. At her house, with some audacity, he rang the bell, but no one answered. He went round to the side street and climbed a nearby tree, peering through the windows, and saw that the rooms were empty. After a while, he went back to the gates of the house and waited. He could do nothing else. Eventually, the housekeeper took pity on him and came out and said that the family had moved to America and would not be coming back. She turned to go back inside again but then paused, as if considering something. Then she turned back to my uncle and said that she had been unsure whether to tell him this next thing, but neverthe-less had decided now that she would. She said that as they had been leaving the girl had asked for a message to be given to my uncle, asking for him simply to wait for her, saying that she would one day return. Apart from being poor and uneducated, my mother ex-plained, my uncle also had a heart condition. The doctors had said that he would die as a child but he had not. Even so, he was still too unwell in those days to fly, even if he'd known where in America they had gone, even if he'd had the money. What else could he do, but thank the housekeeper, and return home? He had continued to work and take care of his health and eventually, when he had enough money, he bought a one-bedroom apartment in the neigh-borhood near the girl's house, which had a new family in it now, and he would walk past every now and then. Eventually, my uncle found a different job, and then another and another, ending up at a newspaper. The company asked him if he would like to move cities, to a bigger, better role, but he turned them down. Even though he no longer sold songbirds, he always kept one with him: yellow and small, sometimes scouring markets all over the city to find the right one. He never married, and had no family. Eventually, my mother said, they received a letter. It was from overseas, in a pale blue inter-national envelope bordered in red and navy. The letter inside was written in a neat and steady hand, and its contents outlined a life lived in strange parallel: an arrival in a new country, a new school, homesickness and heartache that gradually became less and less, then university, the unexpected surprise of new love, followed by a job, marriage, and children. The girl, now a woman and a mother, had asked after my uncle, having tracked him down through a chain of mutual acquaintances and wanted to write again, even to call and speak, but my uncle, though he tried several times, never found it in himself to write a proper reply.

Throughout my childhood, my mother had told me a version of this story many times, just as she had told me other stories, of poverty and family and war. Once, as an adult, I asked her again about my uncle, and to show me the pictures she had once spoken of in such detail, but she had frowned and said that nothing like that had ever happened to her brother. She said that he had worked at a stationery shop on their street, not for a man who sold birds at the market, though yes he had a heart condition that had kept him near their childhood neighborhood all his life, and yes he had never married.

I asked my sister about the story, but she said she could not remember it either. Later, she said that it actually sounded a lot like a TV soap opera she had watched once in high school. The next day, she called again and said that she was making for the first time a sweet rice cake that I might remember from our childhood. She had found the recipe in a magazine and had recognized it immediately, even though she had forgotten about the dish for a long time. The ingredients, she said, were deceptively simple: just rice flour, water, some sugar and a little yeast, which she would mix together and steam and then let cool. She had borrowed a large steamer from our mother and was making it now so that her children could try and remember it too. She said again that she did not remember the story our mother had told about our uncle. Her only clear memory of our mother's family was of going back to Hong Kong for our grandfather's funeral, when she was perhaps six or seven. Like so many childhood memories, this was made up largely of impressions and strong feeling. She remembered sleeping in a strange bed, with a light pink chrysanthemum blanket, the same texture as a towel, knowing that someone, a second cousin or an in-law, had given it up for her, without ever knowing exactly who. The house was constantly filled with people, sitting and chatting or moving freely in and out of the kitchen, at home in a way she was not. My sister said she had found this disorienting as a young child, unable to tell strangers from family members, many of whom were kind to her in sudden and inexplicable ways. They would often come to offer her something, a sweet or a snack, and try and talk to her in Cantonese, which she neither spoke nor understood. They knew this, but still they would try, as if comprehension might come magically, so long as both speakers willed it. My sister would stare back at them blankly, and eventually everyone would give up, shaking their heads and walking away. She knew only a smattering of phrases and for the whole trip was only able to express herself by saying things that meant something like *yes*, *no* and *thank you*. Unlike the other children, she did not seem to know enough to be permitted to help, and instead was both indulged and left alone. She spent most of her time curled up on a rosewood chair, playing her cousin's Game Boy or else watching cartoons on the TV. If she wanted to go outside to play in the small courtyard, to see, for example, the stone lion that stood there, with a ball rolled under its heavy, decorative paw, she was lent a pair of pink flip-flops that were several sizes too big for her, and that had already been worn down and browned with the shape of someone else's feet. The only task she was given was to help with the washing of the rice, repetitively filling and draining the milky liquid until it was almost clear, something simple enough for even a child to do. At night, she would lie awake, listening to the sound of the fans and the rest of the family speaking in the big room.

She said that she did not remember the funeral, only the cemetery, somewhere high up on the hills, filled with gray stone tablets and many, many steps. She said that throughout the whole trip she had been deeply adrift. She had felt watched, and while she was regarded with kindness, this was the sort of leniency that you would allow a small animal, one who did not know any better, who was unable to control its nature. She did not know how to behave, how to navigate the new and complex family strata she had found herself in. Unlike in our small family, there was never time to be alone, never a time to rest. Everyone always seemed busy doing something for someone else, and it made her feel useless and in the way. She knew that the family was grieving, but the man whose photo sat upon the altar in the house and to whose grave they went was a stranger to her. She remembered only the look of the paper money that they had brought that day, because it had come in bright purple packaging, almost magenta, with characters in gold leaf. Against the gray of the stones and the concrete steps, the colors had looked garish and almost beautiful. The money itself had been colorful too, like money in a game. Like everyone else, she had lined up and dropped the money into a fire, and it was only when the wind changed direction and the smoke got into her eyes that she had felt tears. For the rest of the day she had been bored and moody, and when she was given a bowl of food to leave as an offering, she had placed it quickly and carelessly upon the stone ledge, a gesture that she knew would have embarrassed our mother there among her relatives and friends. Someone had ended up buying her an ice cream and she had squatted and eaten it in the tall grasses and the humid air.

The next day, they had driven to a jewelry shop in the next neighborhood, where my sister had seen yet another stone lion, as well as a statue she recognized as the goddess of mercy, with her kind face and long fingers. There was too a bowl, made of jade and filled with water. My sister said that at the bottom, two catfish had been carved out of the stone, swimming among reeds and plants, but recessed, so that it looked as if they were really floating in the water. Sometime during the visit, she realized with shame that the family wanted to buy her a gift to take back with her. They took out and spoke about different pieces of jewelry. Some of the jade was white and opaque, or brown and translucent, not unlike the darkened century eggs that they had been eating in the days before. Others were a deep, creamy green, and reminded her of the mountain peak or the moss that grew at the graveyard. Eventually though, my sister had chosen not jewelry, but something that was more like a toy. On the counter, there was a stack of what looked like tiny books or boxes, with green and blue cloth covers, tied together with red ribbon. When you opened the covers, there was inside a small gold turtle, placed together with a rock, behind a pane of glass. Somehow, as soon as the box was open, the turtle's hands and feet began to move and flutter, its tiny head turning side to side. My sister had fallen in love with this trinket, and somehow having it seemed to appease all the strangeness and confusion she had felt over the past couple of days. Back at the house, especially during crowded meals and visiting times, she would steal away to open the box, and watch as the tiny turtle performed its reliable dance, looking as if it were swimming, even though in reality it was going nowhere at all. On the return journey, she had packed it carefully, folding it between some of her T-shirts, but when she opened it again, she found that the glass, which was secured with a cheap glue, had become displaced, and that the turtle was no longer able to move.

My sister said that she had gone back to Hong Kong only once, when she was a young resident, for a medical conference being held at a hotel in Kowloon. She had hardly recognized the place, and indeed it felt to her like she was visiting for the first time, rather than the second. She had not expected, she said, the strange juxtaposition of the city, its huge gray skyscrapers against the lushness of the subtropical forest, the green mountain peaks, the bay. It was surprisingly beautiful, and she found it hard to believe that she had been there before. By then she had finished medical school, and was working at a busy public hospital, which tested her and which she knew would give her what she needed to specialize. She was doing well, and now had been invited to speak at this well-regarded conference on endocrinology in a foreign city. She barely remembered the awkward, stubborn child she had been when she was there last, the one who was unable to fend for herself, and who had flung the offerings so callously at the grave. For the conference, she had packed a gray, cinch-waisted suit jacket with matching wide-legged pants, under which she wore a simple white crew neck. The auditoriums were dark, crowded. The speakers were good and challenging. She knew that she would improve from having been there. At the entrance, they had given her a lanyard with her name and the name of the hospital on it.

In the evening, she skipped the usual drinks and socializing to see the city, deciding not to bother with the trains, but catching taxis, or the Star Ferry. As the boat had crossed Victoria Harbour, she had taken off her jacket and folded it carefully over the railings at the prow. The wind had pulled at her hair, which she had pinned up that morning, causing short, loose strands to flutter about her face in a way that felt somehow freeing. The sea was choppy and flat, and she had leaned with her forearms over her folded jacket, looking ahead to a city that was shrouded in a fine, golden late-afternoon mist.

She had meant, she said, to get in touch with the rest of the family there, but she had been so busy working before the trip she had run out of time. Once there, she again reminded herself that she would, but first she wanted to have some time just to herself. She had studied and worked so hard all year and now she wanted to indulge. She had met, at the conference, the man who would later become her husband, a young graduate, hardworking and capable, just like herself. He shared too the manner she had acquired over the many years of study, authoritative and empathetic while at the same time being comfortingly impersonal. He too had family close by, in Taiwan, and, like her, had no plans yet to see them. Now, as her husband, he was so familiar to her that she could barely picture a time when she was not deeply accustomed to him, when she might have started at his presence in a room. But she remembered, or at least thought she remembered, the heady days they had spent together, when they did not fully know each other yet. On their day off, they had climbed the sun-drenched Peak. At the top, there had been binoculars stationed at the lookout, and they had done the tourist thing and put coins into the slots to see the city below. On her way up, my sister remembered that she had noticed a pavilion with small stone plinths every few paces and, at the top of each one, another gray stone lion.

The next day, they went to Lantau Island where they caught the glass-bottomed cable car and saw the giant bronze Buddha at the top of the many steps. He waited for her while she shopped for clothes on Canton Road, and that night, they got lost in a warren of tiny bars and restaurants where she was often served drinks for free. Somewhere during these activities, my sister said, she had come to realize that this was a man she could see herself with. Here was someone who, like her, was committed, and from the way he spoke and the things he said, she could sense that he valued stability, that he had planned a certain steady course in life. Like someone who had looked thoroughly at the tests and the patient's history, and now had before them the definitive scan or X-ray, she was relatively confident of the results, the conclusion foregone.

For some reason, in an early conversation, she had let him believe that this too was her first time in Hong Kong. And indeed it was easier, and she had to admit better, to play the tourist, to enjoy the city in this way. She did not mention her family, somewhere—she still did not know exactly where—in the city, and by the time the conference was ending, she told herself that it was now too late. Years later, she said, she still had not clarified this to her husband, though she remembered looking through the binoculars at the peak, wondering, for a brief moment, if her eye would alight, by chance, on the cemetery where she had been so many years before.

On her last day, during a break between talks, she had drifted into a huge department store via an open-air escalator. There was, on the highest, quietest floor, a jewelry shop, where items were displayed on white silk in brightly lit glass cases, and where staff stood dressed in gray suits and white gloves, as if to attention. My sister had bent over the display cabinets, and when she had rested her hand on top, she had heard the gentle, satisfying clink of her gold watch against the glass. Once she had made it clear that she did not speak Cantonese, the man behind the counter switched to English. My sister knew that she did not have much time before she had to be back at the conference, but somehow she also knew that she would buy something from this shop, to remember the trip, just as she had been gifted something during the last. Eventually, she settled on a flat jade disc, more white than green, an abstract shape fixed to a silver torque that lay flat against her skin when she wore it. It reminded her of the old money that had been used once in China, and later, the *bi* discs that were used in ancient funerals, during a time when it was believed that jade would stall the decomposition of the body beneath the earth.

The one place I wanted to get to that day was a church, reportedly a very beautiful building, designed by a famous architect, in a suburb near Osaka. I said to my mother that even though I knew she did not believe in that religion, visiting was supposed to be a profound experience, and I hoped it would be worth the time. Earlier on the train, while lost in thoughts of my uncle and Hong Kong, I had looked over to see my mother's head tilted against the headrest near the window, her eyes fully closed. We left our bags in lockers at the station and switched to the local lines. On the way, we stopped at a small noodle restaurant for lunch. There was a short queue outside, but they served everyone quickly and efficiently, with the capability and speed of a place that had been around for many years, making only the one thing. The noodles came in a large bowl, white on the inside but decorated with a complicated, dense pattern of dull, watermelon pinks and greens and yellows on the outside. It reminded me of the bowls I had often seen in restaurants during my childhood. This same pattern must once have existed on elaborate plates and tableware during a certain period in history. And, much like the famous Qinghua porcelain, it would have been admired and prized, such that when trade first opened up between Asia and the West, it was at first bought, and then replicated, in many different countries, by many different hands, and existed now, in this version, made in a factory and used all over the world, numbering in the hundreds of thousands.

It had been cold outside and warm in the train, and afterward the soup made us both a little sleepy. We walked down suburban streets, with wooden telegraph poles and power lines crisscrossing above. The streets were so small that there were often no footpaths but rather white lines drawn on the asphalt to indicate where you could walk. Occasionally, we'd pass a cluster of convenience stores and small shops and coffee houses, which you could always spot at a distance by their brightly colored vertical signs. At the outdoor museum the other day, we'd drifted by a wooden house where music was playing. My mother had slowed and, seeing that she wanted to go in, I'd turned around and led us through the door. Inside, two women were bent over long instruments. My mother said excitedly that they were Japanese zithers, not unlike the Chinese ones she remembered listening to on the radio as a little girl. I too recognized the sound, deep and woody at times, at others flat and disjointed, or rippling as when you ran your fingers rapidly over the keys of a piano. The women wore three *tsume* on the fingers of their right hands, which looked like white, finely shaped claws or nails, and with which they plucked at the instruments' strings. My mother looked on, fascinated, listening for a long time, and as we left she asked if we could buy a CD of the music while we were there.

I had some trouble at first finding the church, but eventually we came across it, a low, boxlike building in a quiet neighborhood, and entered. Inside, the walls were made of raw concrete, which absorbed most of the light, making the interior dim and gray. The floor was not flat, but sloped ever so slightly downward, as if pulling everything toward the simple southern altar. On the wall behind the altar, two great cuts had been made, one from floor to ceiling and the other horizontally, so that they resembled a giant cross. As we sat, all our attention was focused on this large shape and the brilliant, white light that streamed through the gaps, in contrast to the subdued atmosphere of the room. The effect was riveting, not unlike staring out at the daylight through the opening of a cave. And perhaps, I said to my mother, this too was what it had felt like to be in the earliest churches, when nature itself was still a force in the world, visceral and holy. I said also that the architect had originally intended the cross to be unsealed, so that air and weather would have gusted through the openings, like the will of god itself.

It was a gray, cold day and we were the only two people in the room. I asked my mother what she believed about the soul and she thought for a moment. Then, looking not at me but at the hard, white light before us, she said that she believed that we were all essentially nothing, just series of sensations and desires, none of it lasting. When she was growing up, she said that she had never thought of herself in isolation, but rather as inextricably linked to others. Nowadays, she said, people were hungry to know everything, thinking that they could understand it all, as if enlightenment were just around the corner. But, she said, in fact there was no control, and understanding would not lessen any pain. The best we could do in this life was to pass through it, like smoke through the branches, suffering, until we either reached a state of nothingness, or else suffered elsewhere. She spoke about other tenets, of goodness and giving, the accumulation of kindness like a trove of wealth. She was looking at me then, and I knew that she wanted me to be with her on this, to follow her, but to my shame I found that I could not and worse, that I could not even pretend. Instead I looked at my watch and said that visiting hours were almost over, and that we should probably go.

For the next leg of our journey, I had planned a walk along an old trail, through forests and towns and mountains that had once joined the imperial cities. But I soon realized that this was impossible. It had been raining all week, and the trails would be muddy and wet. My mother had not brought proper hiking shoes like I had asked her. I wanted to push her to do the walk with me, but I realized that this would have been almost cruel. Her face had changed since the times I had seen her last. She had always been youthful, so much so that I realized this was tied very closely to my image of her. Yet during the trip, I would look at her profile, her face when it was tired or resting, and realize that she was now a grandmother. Then, just as quickly, I would forget this again, seeing only the same image of her as I had throughout my childhood, which was strangely fixed, only to have this broken again some days later. I said to her that instead, if she did not mind, I would walk the trail alone, which would separate us for one day and one night. She could stay at a small traditional inn, very near the station. The town was big, but, if she stayed within a certain radius, she should have enough to see without needing to venture far. I would take the train further, and then, over the course of the next day, walk back toward her, returning by evening.

At the inn, I filled a small pack with clothes, rolling each one of them tightly so that they would take up as little space as possible. Then I packed a gas camping stove and a large water bottle, as well as a light raincoat, and left the rest of my luggage with my mother. I asked if she would like to have some tea with me before I left, and we sat on the floor with a black iron teapot between us, which was heavy and hot and pleasant to lift and pour. The room smelt of smoke and newly burnt rice. I said that I had been thinking a little on what she had said the day before, about goodness. I asked her if she remembered the first job I had had, at the Chinese restaurant in a suburb near the river, where I worked during my first year of university. It had been a beautiful restaurant, once famous in fact, and though dated, it still retained some of this aura, with dim, carefully lit rooms and dark polished floors. Inside, everything was done with a certain formality, a certain sense of weight and precision, as if to create a floating world. Our uniforms were black aprons and black shoes, and an ivory-colored shirt with cloth buttons and a small mandarin collar, just enough to give a vague sense of what was once referred to as the Far East. We had been instructed to wear light makeup every night, and to put our hair up, which I did, carefully and precisely, before each shift. The other waitresses were all women in their early twenties and thirties, and at the time they had seemed to me to be impossibly and uniquely adult. I remember that it was expected that we would work hard, and that we would take the reputation of the restaurant seriously, as if its fame could be sustained a little while longer, if only we all believed in it, like a religion, or a faith.

I said that she might also remember my boyfriend at the time, who was another student, studying the same course as me. Like me, he had a sister, and I knew, in some vague way, because he never really spoke about it, that in his childhood they had been poor. He was dedicated and had a chiseled face that seemed too youthful, but that I knew would only become better as he aged. He always worked hard at his studies and went to the gym regularly, and nothing about him offended me, and yet, I felt like we were essentially strangers. He often said too, in an affectionate way, that I was a little strange, and had remarked once in passing that I took my job at the restaurant too seriously. I disagreed, but I had not contradicted him at the time. Back then, I took everything seriously. I studied hard because I genuinely believed it would serve a higher purpose, and I liked the idea of living according to a certain strictness or method. I wanted only to master one thing well in my life. I worked at the restaurant the same way. Before each shift, I always pinned back my hair very tightly. I did this not because I wanted to, but because I felt that I had somehow understood that this style, elegant and strict, suited our role, which was to be contained and capable at all times. In the same way, I found myself doing many small things differently there, as if the very act of crossing through the doors had transformed me, as if I was now porous, or mute. I made a concentrated effort to be efficient and elegant, conscious of my gestures, my voice, the expression on my face, and understanding that if something broke, if we were to drop a tray or plate or stack of glasses, that it would be terrible, almost as if we had deliberately smashed it ourselves in a moment of madness or protest. The restaurant sometimes held large banquets, during which we had to carry long wooden boats topped with seafood and ice, and garnished with vegetables carved into the shape of flowers, which I always wanted to grab and eat, like a child. Though these trays were heavy and unwieldy I made it look easy, holding in my mind the image of a ballet dancer who puts all her weight on the tips of her toes but shows no pain. My boyfriend often joked that I was the kind of person who would be happy in a mountain temple, told only to sweep the dust from the floor each day, to contemplate the nature of time and labor, and the difference, or absolute sameness, between a dirty surface and a clean one.

It was around this time too that I took up swimming again, which I had done regularly as a child. There was an outdoor pool near the restaurant, fifty meters, next to a community center and a park. I bought a black swimsuit, the simplest cut I could find, like a leotard, some goggles and a membership. At first, it had been difficult. I could not believe that my body had nearly forgotten how to swim, something that had seemed almost instinctive when I was younger. But gradually, slowly, with work, it all came back. I went three times a week without fail, even if I was tired, even when the weather was bad or when I had exams. Some days, with the light making hexagons on the bottom of the pool, the sun, the lawns, the absolute clearness of the water, there was no place as beautiful. And if I was in the right mindset, both focused and relaxed, I was able to pull through the water with hardly any effort, with a speed that felt like a close approximation to flying. Walking back from the pool on those days, after having swum, with the gardens and trees in full burst, the sun on the footpath, I felt something—my body as my own, strong and tan, which could be anything I wanted it to be, so long as I worked hard enough. And I felt myself in an instant, the world opening up as if through a great funnel, going from my feet to the leaves to the sky above. In those moments I thought nothing, or if I thought at all it was unnameable. These moments never lasted; they were gone as quickly as they had come, so quickly I could never be sure that they had even happened. And then I had to be on my way.

Shortly after we first met in class, my boyfriend asked if I liked movies. I said yes, and he said that next time he would lend me some of his. At a lecture the following week, he gave me a plastic bag, handling it very carefully and holding it at the bottom as if it were a wrapped gift. I looked inside and saw they were DVDs, mostly action movies, as well as a few romances. They were not classics but rather were from a few years back, so that they seemed both a little dated and yet not old enough. I said thank you, but in truth I had little interest in these kinds of films and did not know what to do with them. In the end, I put them in my bag and left them there, so that they traveled with me for a while wherever I went. After about a week, I returned them without having watched any. My boyfriend asked if I had liked the movies and, not knowing what to say, but seeing the expression on his face, I lied and said yes.

When we had been going out for a year, he planned a dinner for us at a well-known French restaurant, the kind of place that he said he would go to without a second thought after graduation, when he was finally earning real money. I bought a new dress, took the night off work, and got ready at home. While I was doing my hair, I received a message on my phone from a customer at the restaurant. I had not quite understood at first, thinking that either it was a mistake, or the wrong number, or that I was misreading what was there. It also took me some time to place it, to work out who it was from. I saw many customers over the course of each shift, and each time I was able to be completely present with them, before forgetting them with equal completeness once they had left. I would behave slightly differently, make minor changes to my face or my actions according to what was needed, like a subject posed before a photographer, sensitive to the angle or the placement of the light. If a customer wanted to talk, I could be engaged. I listened carefully and steered them subtly toward placing the right order, saying a few simple things in return. If they wanted to be left alone, I was capable too of being calm and quick. I could collect their various plates and bowls in a way that was less about service and more about ceremony, which in turn alleviated the excruciating agony of one person essentially cleaning up after another. I remembered this man coming in, often early, when the restaurant was still poised, almost setting up. He always chose a seat at the corner, with a full view of the floor. I remembered too that he usually came to eat alone, but did not behave like a man who was completely comfortable doing so: meaning that he had always wanted to talk. I think he had hinted that he was in business, and had had some rogue success. I could not remember much more.

When I met my boyfriend outside the French restaurant, I saw that, like me, he had dressed up, and was wearing a white shirt and dark pants, not unlike my uniform at work. We went inside and were seated and handed the menus. At the table, my boyfriend's profile as he glanced at the wine list was like an ad for an expensive watch. I knew that for him this night was already a success. He had done something he felt to be romantic, something correct and good and this, rather than the cost of the meal, was his gift to me. It was a gesture that, in his mind, moved us along together, progressed us to some higher state, like a broom pushing two stones forward along a path. I felt, on some level, that I should be happy too. I ended up ordering what I felt was the wrong thing, but when my boyfriend asked me how the food was, I did not say that I thought it was in a way, dishonest, dressing up the flavors until you could hardly tell it was food any longer. I was conscious of how important it was to enjoy this meal, or at least to seem to enjoy it. I thought that if I tried hard enough my effort would become real happiness, and then I would finally be able to stop having these thoughts. When dessert came, it was a kind of flambé. We broke the crust of the meringue with our spoons and inside it was so sweet and sugary it made me feel like falling asleep. I had the vague thought I had been taught somehow that the best thing was still to be desired, even if you did not desire, even if you did not much like the person who desired you. Where I had learned this, I did not yet know.

The rest of the semester unfolded in a familiar pattern. I swam, I studied together with my boyfriend in the library. I went to class. My sister was doing a placement in a hospital in the country, and when she came back to visit, we went to Chinatown and did all the things we used to do when we were at school: eating spicy dumplings at the restaurant in the cobbled alleyway, watching an old martial arts movie in the cool dark of the cinema, buying cheap snacks from the store next door. At the restaurant, I continued to work as I had always done, being careful, attentive, setting up the tables and preparing the rooms. If the customer came in and I happened to be rostered to his section, I continued to take his orders and he continued to make small talk as if nothing had happened. Neither of us ever acknowledged the messages he had sent me. And yet, the knowledge of it was there. One day, when I had taken some time off to study for exams, he messaged to say that he hadn't seen me in a while, and asked if I was okay. Another time, he wrote about his divorce, and his young son, whom I had seen with him once, and mentioned too in passing his wife, whom I had never seen, but who he said was Chinese. He said that he had recently started to paint, and though his words were modest I felt somehow that he wanted me to acknowledge his talent, or at least its potential. I recalled that we might have once briefly spoken about art, or literature, or film, because of something I was studying. I asked the manager if anyone at the restaurant might have given my phone number out, and he looked at me like I was crazy. The manager said that I was a hard worker, that the owners appreciated me, and that he hoped everything was going well with my degree. I thought about how strange it was that the only two people who knew about what was happening were the man and myself, and how, for some reason, the most important thing to me right then was only the ability to pretend that it was not happening at all.

My boyfriend invited me to an exhibition of paintings at the city's largest gallery. We went after class one day, catching the tram down and disappearing into a dark stone building surrounded by fountains. Inside, it was teeming with people in wide spaces. Some of the ceiling was glass and a cold, white light streamed down. I was feeling tired and a little bored, but we went and got our tickets and checked our backpacks into the cloakroom, and then headed up the narrow escalators. At first, my boyfriend and I drifted together past the works, which he admired and called beautiful, though I had a feeling he did not know exactly why. It was as if we were inspecting a row of pearls, which of course were beautiful by their very nature, so that simply to say so meant close to nothing. Eventually, I went ahead, and came to a room with a painting by Monet, the same one, I said to my mother, that I had seen with her earlier that week. Pausing, I reached for the teapot between us and refilled both our cups, even though my mother had barely taken a sip, while mine was nearly empty.

I said that I knew very little of Monet, both then as a student, and now. I did not know much about the era in which he had painted, or the famous techniques he had pioneered. But in that moment in the city gallery with my boyfriend, looking at the pale light, the great shapes of hay in a field, something had struck me. They had seemed to me then, as now, like paintings about time. It felt like the artist was looking at the field with two gazes. The first was the gaze of youth, awakening to a dawn of pink light on the grass, and looking with possibility on everything, the work he had done just the day before, the work he had still to do in the future. The second was the gaze of an older man, perhaps older than Monet had been when he painted them, who was looking at the same view, and remembering these earlier feelings and trying to recapture them, only he was unable to do so without infusing them with his own sense of inevitability. Looking at them, I felt a little like I felt sometimes after reading a certain book, or hearing a fragment of a certain song. The moment seemed too linked to those afternoons walking back from the pool after I had taken up swimming again, to the wideness of the world. I felt that if only I could connect these things better, then I might truly have come to realize something. Then my boyfriend came to stand beside me, and remarked on this painting as he had remarked on all the others. I said nothing. Instead, I thought about how kind we always were to each other, how we had never once in our entire relationship fought or even openly disagreed. I thought of how people had so often described my manner as gentle, or how customers at the restaurant would sometimes praise the staff as they tipped, remarking on the elegance of the waitresses, their soft voices, their accommodating ways.

At the restaurant, we had one of our busiest nights of the year. The back rooms were filled, the floor packed. I was working the banquet section with another girl, which meant working to coordinate a large set menu in pairs. During these times, you had to work quickly, clearing each course when it was done and laying out a new one, remembering the exact combination of plates and colors. Meanwhile you had to pay attention to the time, making sure to call out the orders to the kitchen correctly: too early and the courses would crash into each other, disrupting the flow, and too late and the diners would get hungry and restless. Midway through the night, I passed the table where the man was sitting, this time with a friend, and he made a gesture to stop me, and for some reason, I stopped, even though I had meant to ignore it. He asked for another beer and I took the old bottle from the table and wrote the order down. As he spoke, I remembered thinking back to when he had first come to the restaurant, which might have been around the time of his divorce, eager to talk about his business, his art. I could not remember what I had said then, how I had acted, but I remembered that I had felt sorry for him. It might have been that out of sympathy I had smiled, and said some simple things, things which he had taken to mean the opposite of what I had meant them to be. The man spoke for a long time, even though he could see the restaurant was busy, even though he could see I had to go. Next to him, his friend, whom I had never seen before but who resembled the man in ways that were more emotional than physical, said nothing, but laughed occasionally, his face turning pink from the beer, and continued to watch, as if he were the audience at a fascinating play. I held the empty beer bottle in my hand and listened, all the while thinking about the other waitress on her own at the back of the restaurant, the plates she must be juggling, the orders I must be missing. I could not understand how the man was unable to tell the difference between my actions and my feelings, which were so strong and pure by then that I could feel them radiating from me like some kind of heat. When he finally stopped talking, I went back to the kitchen and put the empty bottle in the recycling. I could not explain it at the time, but I felt that he had taken something, something that touched on the privacy of my happiness at the pool, or the brink of what I had felt looking at the painting. These things were precious, and they were still mysteries to me, and now, I knew, I was further from them. I pushed my hair back and knelt to take a tray and a cloth to wipe down the table. Then I got up and went back to the banquet room, where we were now badly behind, and began to help in there.

As soon as the train left the station, I felt a sense of relief. I wanted to walk in the woods and among the trees. I wanted not to speak to anyone, only to see and hear, to feel lonely. The train passed by fields and farms, plastic-covered greenhouses and small crossings. A little way along, I got off and bought fruit and some balls of rice and seaweed, as well as tea and crackers from a convenience store. Then I caught the bus up the mountain, to the beginning of the trail. I would stay overnight at the inn, before walking back in the direction I had come in the morning. On the way, I had seen that there was a bathhouse not far from where I was staying, and I took a towel with me and left the rest of my things and made my way back down the road. It was late afternoon, and while walking, I did not see a single car. The bathhouse was a wooden structure at the end of a dirt path. The trees around it were a deep green, a thick, dark mulch of mud and earth and fallen foliage on the ground. The bath was deep, the water cloudy. I washed and wrapped my hair up above my head before entering. The walls were made out of heavy stone and the wooden floors were wet and shiny, the boards long and long-ago stained black. There was no one else there and no one came the whole time I stayed.

Outside, I could see the day darkening. There were two long, stretched squares of white light on the surface of the water, reflections from the window. I thought of my afternoons at the pool when I had been a student, how I had felt, long and lean. I thought of my mother, who had never learned to swim, and of Laurie, and of kayaking across the crater lake near where he'd grown up.

Earlier this year, we had moved cities together, and bought an apartment near the deep bowl of the bay. So far, we'd had one winter there: short days, the strongest winds we had ever felt, but everything still new. Sometimes, it felt like we were two climbers who had come up to a plateau, quiet, awed, and a little stunned to have finally found a place of rest. I thought of the mornings there, when I would doze, often listening to the sounds of Laurie getting ready for work: the percolator on the stove, the shower running, the smell of coffee, his boots on the wooden floors. If the cat came in, I would hear first the gentle tacking of her feet, and then feel the weight of her as she lay across my chest, purring so deeply I could feel the tremor in my own throat. I liked the apartment. The front room had a view of the bay. You could undo the latch and slide back the glass door, which had a row of small white squares across the face, faded and peeling, and look out to a sea that, in the first few months, had been gray like the rain, or pale like the edge of a blue cup. Most of the rooms had two doors, and you could walk in a circular fashion from the front room to the kitchen to the hallway and then to the bedroom, almost like a theater set. From any room, you were always seeing the suggestion of another, as in a painting where the subject gazes into a mirror, looking at something just out of sight. I liked most of all the days when I could wander about barefoot, never even needing to leave the apartment. The carpet was a dense, old blue, the color of a Russian gray, laid tightly across the stairs like folded paper. In the kitchen, there were old floorboards that felt soft and creaking and warm. I'd go from room to room, vaguely tidying as I went. There were books left open on the floor, cups, newspapers, our jackets and clothes, blankets unfolded and drawn into corners or slung over chairs. I'd bring the cups and plates into the kitchen and wash them while looking out into the small patch of garden, where the weeds grew freely. Or I'd take a cloth and wipe down the table, the shelves, picking up briefly the rock Laurie had brought back once from the mountain, the one that looked like a man's nose in profile, the one that he had held in his hand even as we scrambled over boulders and picked our way along the river edge aided by ropes. There were always small changes: an orange that had gone soft in the fruit bowl, lists of things on scrap paper. We once brought back a huge leathery brown pod from the bush and put it in the kitchen, near the oven, the warmest place. One morning, we woke to find that it had opened, revealing a seed as big and dark as the pit of an avocado.

Another time, the power cut out and we dug up a headlamp and a few candles from one of the still-unpacked moving boxes. While the storm went on outside, we went round and placed the candles at various guiding points throughout the house. When I lit them in the kitchen, it smelled briefly of birthday cakes. I remember cooking a simple dinner, pulling the skins off the tomatoes in the near darkness, going by feel rather than by sight. Laurie had put the record player on, and danced slowly and achingly in front of the cat, who continued to glower from her cushion on the floor. We could barely see the food on the table, noticing only the shapes and textures of the vegetables in their bowls. I had taken the washing in and sheets were hung and draped over the rack, a ladder, a glass door. Outside, we could hear that the wind was strong, but inside, it was still. I remembered thinking, as we ate, how such happiness could come from such simple things.

In April, we'd gone to visit Laurie's father, flying up north first and then renting a small, bright yellow car and driving for several hours. It had been near the end of the wet season, and everything was lush and green. I looked out the window at the flat roads and the low hills and the great, stormy skies, fascinated to see the landscape that Laurie had grown up in, and which must have been, in some way, a part of him still. Laurie, I knew, was both happy and unhappy to be back in the place he had left as a teenager, and for some reason I felt like I was seeing something private, as if he were suddenly a boy again, and I was looking at a part of him that he had long ago abandoned. On the way, we stopped so that we could switch drivers and Laurie had taken a photo of me standing next to the bright yellow car in a field of green sugarcane. As we drove, he pointed out his old high school, the house of a childhood friend, the beaten track where he'd trained and competed as a kid. We stopped at a large lake, which seemed to be an almost perfect circle. Laurie explained that the lake had been formed by a crater, and that no one knew how deep it really was. He'd swum across it many times as a teenager, and once, he and his first girlfriend had borrowed a friend's canoe and taken a tent and camped on the other side.

His father lived on a large, fertile inland property. They had built out most of the house around the original weatherboard themselves, adding a spare room, where we stayed, and a large wooden deck. There was a hutch for the guinea pigs, and in the mornings a rooster strutted and crowed among the hens and the cut grass. Even though he had not lived there for many years, Laurie moved around with a deep sense of familiarity, the kind that could only come from childhood. He went freely from room to room, picking up objects like he owned them, knowing all the paintings on the walls and where everything was kept. In the spare room, he found a shoebox full of old photos, and showed me one of his fifth birthday party, all the boys dressed up as pirates, hanging off a wooden ship his father had built for them, and that had stayed in the garden for many years. His father offered us coffee and fruit, something green and nutty, with a custard-like consistency, and they spoke about the old house and Laurie's siblings and his father's work. Later, his father said, he would take us to the hanger to see the light plane that he sometimes flew, and if we wanted and if the weather held, we could go up with him while we were there.

We'd got up early the next morning and hiked to a place in the mountains that Laurie knew, where he said we could swim. Even at that hour, the sun had been hot, but Laurie said that once we got to the track, it would be all right, we would be under the cover of the trees. I said that the night before, I had dreamed of the crater lake. He had been a teenager again and I had been his girlfriend at the time. I said that we had swum out together easily but when we reached the middle, I had stopped and said that I couldn't do it, that I couldn't go on. I remembered the feeling of the endless depth beneath me, which I could only feel because he had told me about it, thinking that if I stopped now I would sink and sink and no one would know for how long. But in the dream, Laurie had said no, go on, and then we had, and when we reached the other side, it was night.

When we got to the path, I saw that Laurie had been right: the trees formed a dense canopy overhead and the shade was thick and lush. The path had been very steep and Laurie had gone first. I remembered following his long, confident strides, going up over roots and rocks. He had climbed this path, and others, many times, and knew them well enough that he did not need to think. This whole world, on the other hand, was both beautiful and deeply unfamiliar to me. After a while, I heard the sound of the river next to us, and though I could not see it at first through the trees, the sound of the water was as soothing as singing. At one point, Laurie stopped and gestured toward something ahead of us. Between the trees, right in the middle of the path, there was a web, a giant orbed spider near its center. Wordlessly, we ducked around it. Eventually, I was able to see the river beside us, and not long after, Laurie brought us to a bank where we could swim. There, the water was cool and brown and clear. I stood on the sand and saw tiny schools of fish gathered in the shallows. On the other side, a giant cliff rose up at an angle. Its gray ridges hung over the water, full of dark mouths and seams, worn back in places to a color that was almost pink. The rocks, where they met the water, were dark and green, and smelled of minerals. Laurie opened his backpack and handed me some fruit, which he must have picked from his father's trees that morning. We ate breakfast, and then we took off our clothes and swam.

Later in the day, Laurie's father took us to his studio, a large timber and corrugated iron shed. All around were tools, equipment, plastic sheets, and a low table, close to the floor, where you could eat or read. His father had pointed to some of the things he was working on: a portrait of a friend, whose face he had been attempting to sculpt for years, unsatisfied, until he'd finally got it right, and another of an abstract female figure, at once heavy and light, in bronze. The male face, I thought, was somehow both certain and formless, as if he had done only the minimal amount in order to summon something. The place for the eyes was cast in shadow, such that they could have been open or closed, the lips firm and downturned. His father, I noticed, spoke easily and gently, much like Laurie did. Earlier, he had pointed out the wild orchids growing in the cracks in the rocks, and I noticed in him, as with Laurie, the ability to pick out the small details of the world, or to see things that others might miss. It was, I suspected, something he did unconsciously, or automatically, not realizing how it would return later in the sculptures he made, or the things he said. But then again, perhaps he did know, and cultivated it, as one nurtured a new plant.

I opened the shoebox Laurie had found in the spare room, and tipped the contents out onto the bed. Inside, there were more photos, Laurie and his siblings as kids, all of them walking down a dirt road at dusk, somewhere where the landscape looked newly razed and bare, his mother carrying either him or his sister in her arms, a pale moon just visible overhead. There were postcards from people I did not know, a passport with the identification page cut out. I found a drawing that Laurie had done of a fish in water. When I asked him about it, he said it was from primary school, when he was about eleven. I said I did not believe him, that it was too good for an eleven-year-old, and he reminded me that his mother had been a painter, and those were her drawings that hung on the walls.

Laurie spent the afternoon fixing a new window for his father's studio, carefully measuring and planing back the wood so that it would fit, while I read and watched him from the deck. His father cooked a simple green curry for dinner, and we ate outside, shelling prawns as the sky turned violet above us, the timber of the table silvery with age. While we ate, Laurie and his father talked freely. They told stories about surviving cyclones, about traveling across the country together, about accidents and pranks played by the children long ago. These stories, I sensed, were ones that had been told many times, passed around and shaped by the whole family, smoothened and refined with each telling. As I listened, I thought too about Laurie's drawing and his father's sculptures, how they were somehow alive. Earlier, I'd asked his father a little about his work, and he'd spoken about the process, the method of subtraction or addition, how he might choose to make something from wood or stone, depending on its properties, or how he would sometimes create a mold so that he could cast in metal or bronze. I had wanted to ask more, to probe deeper, but somehow I couldn't think of how to phrase what I wanted to know, and so let the moment pass. Laurie and I read till late, and when I finally fell asleep, I sensed that Laurie was no longer reading, but looking at me as one is able to look upon a person one knows well, fully, and without reserve.

I woke early and left in the morning light. There was mist on the mountains, and I noticed too that a fine rain was falling. I took out a waterproof cover and fitted it over my pack, as well as a raincoat. Again, I saw few people. On the road, I stuck to the shoulder and cars passed me with what seemed like gentle caution, as if I were an animal they did not want to startle. The air was cool and damp on my face. I walked through quiet villages with small gardens and houses, where people had dug up vegetables and left them to dry in baskets by the door. I passed by an empty train platform, bridges, a dam where the water rushed down from an invisible source, black and cold while moving, white and strong against the rocks. My pack was heavy with food and water, including the two giant red apples I had found at the grocery store the day before. Around me were country roads and farmland. I walked past a woodshed where the logs had been tightly and neatly stacked. Ahead, some bright fruit was growing on the trees and up closer I saw that they were persimmons. Some were hard and new, while others lay on the ground in a sweet pulp. I dug around in the branches for some ripe ones and picked them to eat as I walked. I thought again of Laurie, and wondered what he would make of this scene now, this walk, what he would speak of and observe. Alone, I could not seem to move my own thoughts. In an email he had said that, when I got back, we could begin work on a wooden rack to hang in my study. From it, we could hang potted plants, so that the room would be like its own little jungle.

Soon, I had left the road and was on the trail. In some places, the path was like a corridor, surrounded by trees on either side, tall and spirit-like, swaying around me as if to a sound I could not hear. The earth smelled cold and rich, like the bottom of a well, and the path wound steeply upward, wet and muddy in places. I passed by a river and two small waterfalls, whose sound was almost indistinguishable from the rain. The water as it poured down the rocks was bright and white, like salt. I thought of nothing and no one. On a rock near my feet, there was a tiny frog, the same color as an autumn leaf. The trail continued to wind through a combination of villages and mountains. I disappeared in and out of the forest like a character in a book. From a house high up on a hill, a medium-size dog, its coloring somewhere between a fox and a coyote, with its tail curved upward, watched me go by. I thought of my mother, and how some day, in the future, I would go with my sister to her apartment, the one I had never seen, with the single task of sorting through a lifetime of possessions, packing everything away. I thought of all the things I would find there—private things like jewelry, photo albums and letters, but also signs of a careful and well-organized life: bills and receipts, phone numbers, an address book, the manual for the washing machine and dryer. In the bathroom, there would be half-used glass vials and jars of creams, signs of her daily rituals that she did not like anyone else to see. My sister, I knew, ever methodical, would suggest we sort things into piles: things to keep, things to donate, things to put in the trash. I would agree but, in the end, I knew I would keep nothing, whether out of too much, or too little sentiment, I did not know.

Sometime in the afternoon, I stopped under a shelter to eat and make tea. I unfolded the tiny stove, the gas bottle an ambulance red, lit the burner, and placed a thin aluminum pot on top. Then I unscrewed the top of one of my water bottles and filled the tin. It was somehow incredible to see the steam rising, the water boiling, amidst the constant patter of the rain. While I had been walking, the movement had kept me warm but now I realized that my hair was slightly wet, as was my sweater. I had bought the raincoat at a secondhand shop before coming, not really expecting it to rain much. It was, I realized now, more like a windbreaker, thin enough so that some rain could get through, and also, I realized, coming apart a little at the shoulder. I decided it didn't matter that much. I was sure the rain was lighter now, and that in any case there was nothing I could do. I drank the tea and ate two of the rice balls, which were delicious, and felt suddenly ravenous. I ate the crackers and one of the apples. When I got up to go ahead, I tried to position the straps of my backpack so that the split in the seam would not get any bigger.

Toward the end of our visit with Laurie's father, we had driven back to the crater lake, rented kayaks and pushed out onto the water. I remembered that the day had been still, the water glass-like. The comet had forged such a deep hole that the trees grew right up to the edge of the water, whose depth dropped quickly and suddenly, so that the whole lake felt perfectly enclosed, in a way that was uncanny and almost artificial. There too it had started, very gently, to rain. I had followed the tail of Laurie's kayak, whose wake had spread in a gentle V, like a guide. I thought again about how no one knew how deep the lake really was, and how I could not stop thinking about this. With the water so calm, with the rain misting the other shore, it was hard to get a real sense of distance, and we paddled further and further, everything floating, as in a dream.

Laurie told me about a time when he and his brother had set out on a kayaking trip, not on this lake, but along a very large river. The trip was meant to take several days, and they'd packed all their food and equipment carefully, dividing the weight equally between each kayak. Laurie said that somewhere along the way, they came to their first set of rapids, which they passed through smoothly. He said that he still remembered that feeling, the ease with which his body had reacted, thinking so fast that it appeared not to be thinking at all, but getting every angle, every drop, just right. He was still basking in that feeling when suddenly, he had gone under—he still did not know why, but perhaps there had been another, secondary set of rapids that he had failed, in his reverie, to anticipate. He said that he remembered being down, the water rushing around his body, his face, his skull, but being oddly calm, thinking only that he should wait, wait and see what would happen next. And then, just as quickly, he was upright again, his brother beside him. For some reason, Laurie had said, after he had managed to cough and gasp and breathe normally again, neither he nor his brother had acknowledged the moment, but instead had calmly gone on, never speaking about it for the rest of the journey, even though he had seen the look on his brother's face when he'd surfaced. I wondered if perhaps it was because it had been too real, too terrible, but Laurie said no, he thought perhaps it was the opposite: that both of them had known it would make no difference, they both wanted to go on, and had no choice but to go on. There would be other rapids that they would have to pass through, and what had happened had not changed that. I remember thinking then about Laurie's drawing, and his father's portrait of his friend, how it seemed to me to have almost come full circle. There was something about his father's sculpture that reminded me of the cliff at the waterfall, or the shape forged by the crater—it almost seemed not to have been made by hand at all. Rather, it was more like a rock that one might glimpse in the near distance: shaped just so by the wind or by rain or by time, such that its shallow angles and shadows represented a face in some inexplicable way, and so was all the more surprising and beautiful, because it was both an accident, and a symbol.

I had asked one day if Laurie's father would mind if I visited his studio again. I remembered that I asked this in the same way my sister's children sometimes asked for things: casually, but in a way that indicated that they had been thinking about their request all day. I left my book on the table and went alone to the timber shed. It was early afternoon and the light had been bright. I remembered shielding my face with my hand as I walked. There was a large rusted metal bolt on the door, but there was no lock for it and so I pulled it back. Inside, it smelled like freshly cut wood. Light came down in shafts through the dirty windows, and the motes stirred in them, like the air from a newly threshed harvest of wheat that Chekhov had once written about in one of his stories. I had walked over to the portrait, feeling for some reason as if I were breaking into a space that I should not be in, and so would have to be quick if I was to get what I finally wanted. Carefully, I had removed the plastic cover, and stood looking at the head of the man. I was short enough so that my face was almost at the same height as his, my nose to his nose, my eyes to his eyes, which were either open or closed, and in this way, we could almost look at each other. I studied the sculpture, wondering all the time if someone would come in and end things before I was ready to. That morning, I had asked Laurie's father to tell me more about his work, and he had spoken about his training in Europe, about how he had first been a math teacher, before transitioning into art. He'd spoken too about the engineering involved, about weight and counterweight, about proportion and curing. But by the end of the conversation, I'd still felt confused. What I really wanted to know was how he had made the face: how exactly had he given it its human quality, and how, for example, had he known to balance so precisely the grave and the opaque? I felt that nothing I had ever done had been alive in this way, but it seemed that I did not even know enough to ask the right questions. I remembered too, in the garden of our home, standing next to Laurie and watching him turn the wood on a lathe, how sure and certain he was as he found a shape for it, and how I had always envied him that.

High in the mountain, a section of the path was laid out with timber boards, thick and old, like the beams on a train track. Up there, it might have been raining for days, and the boards were now green and slippery, covered in what felt like a fine layer of algae. A few were missing in places, showing the ground a meter or so beneath. I made my way up slowly, careful not to slip and fall. There were dense ferns, thin black trunks and in the distance a mist so deep it seemed to be almost mauve against the green. At a few points, I stopped to rest and look at the view. Through the sheets of rain, the landscape looked almost like a screen painting that we had seen in one of the old houses. It had been made up of several panels, and yet the artist had used the brush only minimally, making a few careful lines on the paper. Some were strong and definite, while others bled and faded, giving the impression of vapor. And yet, when you looked, you saw something: mountains, dissolution, form and color running forever downward.

The night before I had been scrolling through my phone, looking at some of the photos from our time in Tokyo. In the midst of shots of rooms and gardens, the ceramics I had photographed at the museum, I came across a twenty-two-second video of me at the Shibuya crossing. Crowds surged around in every direction and commercials played on the giant screens above. The lights were about to change, and through the microphone I could hear my mother's voice telling me to wait, wait and smile. One evening,

I came out of the shower to find her sitting on her bed, her things in an uncharacteristic disarray. She looked at me in a panic and said that she'd lost her passport. I asked her if she was sure and she said she'd looked everywhere, checked all her things twice; it was gone. In just a few days, we'd need to be in Kyoto, before flying back home. I asked her to think back, to focus on the last time she had it. I said that we had one more day in Tokyo, we could call up some places, retrace our steps. If not, I said, we'd have to go to a consulate or embassy. I tried to think of the words in Japanese for what we needed, but my mind went blank. The next day, we went everywhere: to Ueno, Hibiya, Aoyama and Roppongi. The streets were wet and slicked with rain. I kept on glancing at the ground, as if we'd stumble across the passport like a lost earring. Eventually, we went back to the hotel, tired and depleted. Not long after, she gasped, and then turned to me, her face breaking with relief, pulling it out from a hidden pocket in her suitcase.

I thought of how, out of all the places we had seen, she had seemed happiest at a small store we'd found in one of the many underground passages that joined the subway stations. It had been the kind that sold gloves and socks, in such number that they were affordable, and on sale. The store had been crowded, with many people going through the racks. My mother had spent close to forty minutes there, looking through the various sections, and had bought gifts for everyone. She had made sure to choose very carefully and thoughtfully, matching each person to an item as best she knew how, and had bought two sets of brightly colored gloves for my sister's children, as well as a pair for me. Whenever I'd asked her what she'd like to visit in Japan, she'd often said she would be happy with anything. The only question she'd asked once was whether, in winter, it was cold enough for snow, which she had never seen.

On the mountains, I knew I was taking longer than I should. It was getting dark and everything ran, streaming toward the ground. And yet, even in my exhaustion, there was too a kind of sweetness. I thought of Laurie and of our many conversations about children. My lecturer had said to us once that parents were their children's fate, not only in the way of the tragedies, but in many other smaller, yet no less powerful ways as well. I knew that if I had a daughter, she would live partly because of the way I had lived, and her memories would be my memories, and she would have no choice in that matter. When we were younger, my mother had regularly read to us from a book of Japanese fables, having saved nothing from her own childhood. One story had been about a mountain, whose peak was surrounded by a ring of clouds, like a necklace, and who had been so beautiful that the greatest of all mountains had fallen in love with her. But the mountain with the clouds had not returned the other's affections, and instead had pined after a smaller, flatter mountain below. The great mountain had been so shocked and enraged by this, it had erupted into a volcano, covering the skies with smoke and darkness and pain for many days. I remember for some reason feeling incredibly moved by this story, the love of the beautiful cloud mountain for the kinder, smaller one, the torment of the volcano, as if, at that age, their passions had seemed more real to me than any human ones. I could not remember any other story from that book, except for one where a young woman dies in the snow, even though I tried to recall them as I walked.

The evening became a deep blue, the temperature began to cool. I was feeling further and further away from everything. The ferns by the side of the road were almost shadows. I knew I should be going faster, that I should try and outrun the coming night, but, like the day we had spent kayaking across the lake, I could not seem to find any real sense of urgency. Instead I wandered slowly, feeling almost like someone lost, who contemplates simply lying down to sleep where they stand. I passed by an old bridge and stopped to walk across it and saw the water, filled and sped by the rain, pouring down. Finally, I saw the train station in the distance, lit by a low orange light, appearing through the blue of the night as if through a haze. The last train was in forty minutes. I pulled the sleeves of my jacket over my hands and wrapped my arms around myself as I sat on the bench to wait. Eventually, I got up and bought a bottle of sake from one of the vending machines. It was clear and cold, tasting at first of alcohol and something vaguely sweet, before evaporating into nothing. After a while, I was no longer cold, but only very tired. I had one vague, exhausted thought that perhaps it was all right not to understand all things, but simply to see and hold them.

At the inn, my mother was not in our room. I asked at the reception and the man there said that he had not seen her. He even went so far as to say that the room had only been booked for one person, me, not for two. For some reason, this irritated me, and I felt this show itself in the tone of my reply. The inn was so small, and we had both checked in the day before. How could he not recall the number of guests? I went back to our room and waited. Earlier, when taking my shoes off at the entrance, I had realized they were soaked and muddy and that my socks were wet. I knew I should have a shower, put on some dry clothes, but I felt weary. After a while, I went out and stood in the street, looking at first in one direction, and then the other. The lights of the shops and cars seemed to come from nowhere, like a train slowly advancing. When my mother finally appeared, she might as well have been an apparition. She came with her puffer jacket zipped up to her chin, and in the cold night air her breath came out in a little cloud, like a small departing spirit. The lights of a car were behind her. She walked toward me very slowly, with no clear sense of recognition on her face, as if I were the ghost she did not want to meet. In her hands she carried a white supermarket bag. I could smell rice, hot curry. When she recognized me her face broke out with warmth. Here you are, she said, as if we had merely missed each other by minutes, as if she were welcoming me into her home. Come and eat, she said.

That evening, I was tired, almost asleep on my feet. My mother unpacked the curry and rice for us and we ate together. While I showered, she unrolled the futons and made up the beds, and when I came back passed me a pair of thick woolen socks. They were very large and new and bright red, and for some reason this made me laugh. Outside, the wind gusted and rattled the windowpanes. We could both hear the deep swells of rain expanding and contracting. I checked my phone and saw that there were reports of a typhoon heading toward Tokyo, and fell asleep with the storm in my ears.

The next day, I was coming down with a cold, my head heavy, but we had to check out and catch the train to Kyoto, which would be our last stop before flying back home. On the way, I had a sudden craving for a flavor from my childhood: some herb, sweet and bitter, like star anise, a black root the color of seaweed, that I could taste in my imagination, but, like so many things, that I could no longer name. On the train, my mother passed me her phone and I read out our horoscopes, predicting love, caution, money and luck, all in the same month. The food and drinks cart came by and I bought two green tea ice creams, even though it was perhaps a little too cold to eat them, and handed one to my mother. The taste was bitter and pleasant, and the ice creams in their soft paper cups, with their small, flat wooden spoons, reminded me of the very same cups she used to buy for my sister and me when we were young, which she let us eat sitting in the playground while she did the shopping. I remembered how much we had anticipated the ice creams each week, how excited we were when the right day came about, as if that was the only focus, hardly even thinking of all the work involved for my mother. I remembered how Laurie and I had once joked about my frugalness, how I would finish up the leftovers of every meal, even if I was not hungry, how I could not bear to see anything go to waste. At the time, I had joked about it too, but what I had not said was that it was her frugalness, not mine, that I was repeating. She had kept, I knew, all the tickets, brochures and guides we had been given to take home, as if she would take them out later to read as one reads a novel. When my niece and nephew unwrapped their presents, I knew too that she would take the paper before it could be thrown away, so that it could be reused to wrap other gifts at other times.

As we looked out the window, the landscape went by in streaks of white and gray and red. At one point, the tracks swept down toward the coastline, and we followed the sea, which was a flat, milky blue after the storm. My mother looked at me and smiled, as if she was simply happy that we were in each other's company, and to have no need for words. We had said, it seemed, so little of substance to each other these past weeks. The trip was nearly ending, and it had not done what I had wanted it to. I thought of learning Japanese, how childlike I still felt in the language, how I was capable only of asking for the simplest things. And yet, I persisted, because I dreamed one day of being able to say more. I thought of the instances when I had been able to converse in a string of sentences, like with the woman at the bookshop, and how good this had felt, how electric. I wanted more of those moments, to feel fluency running through me, to know someone and to have them know me. I thought too of how my mother's first language was Cantonese, and how mine was English, and how we only ever spoke together in one, and not the other.

My mother's stories—whatever she had, or had not told us

about my uncle, or her early days in a new country. It was not that she had kept these things hidden, or deliberately changed them. I knew, for example, about her brother's heart, or about her first time on an international flight, and the name of the village that her parents had been born in, which too was far away from Hong Kong. But beyond that, there was almost nothing. Her parents, she had said, had spoken little of their own childhoods, and so, as it so often is with distance, things ended with the name of the village. I thought of the movie I had watched on the plane over, a story about a scientist who discovers the secret to time travel, and so jumps ahead to the future, where everything is alien and un-recognizable to her, including her own life. I remembered looking from the movie screen to the window of the plane, where, below, the lights of many small towns glowed like remote settlements. Perhaps, I thought, my sister and I had grown up in a way that must have seemed equally foreign to my mother. Perhaps, over time, she had found the past harder and harder to evoke, espe-cially with no one to remember it with. Perhaps it was easier that way, so much so that after a while this new way became her habit, another thing she grew used to, like eating cereal for breakfast, or keeping your shoes on in other people's homes, or rarely speaking to another in your mother tongue.

In Kyoto, the sun came out for what felt like the first time in weeks. Subconsciously, we turned our faces to it. All that was left of the passing typhoon was a strong, deliberate wind. The next morning, we caught the train to the bamboo forests, which were dense and tall and an almost turquoise blue. The trail was short, and crowded. Around us, people were posing doing karate chops, or else dressed in kimonos and riding in rickshaws, hoping, it seemed, to live as they thought people had once lived, which was a time that didn't really exist at all. Afterward, we visited some of the shrines and gardens and I was surprised to see that my mother knew how to toss money into the wooden box, to ring the bell, clap her hands and pray.

Afterward, we walked the streets of Gion, huddled over against the wind, taking photos in front of the wooden doors and shopfronts and stopping for tempura at a restaurant near one of the famous temples. I came across, by chance, a clothing shop in an alleyway, and beckoned my mother in. The roof was surprisingly high, like an old barn, and smelled lightly of cedar. The clothing was displayed on metal racks or else single hangers, many of which were suspended from the ceiling by thin wires, so that the garments swung ever so slightly when you touched them. Much of the material was colored black and the dye was so inky it reminded me of a paint that I had once read about, one that had been used by an artist in collaboration with some scientists, and was said to be so absolute it absorbed almost all light. Yet the clothes, when you began to look at them, were not absolute at all, but rather made from segments and folds and drapes, such that it was sometimes hard to tell how you would put each piece on. Or perhaps, I thought, there was no correct way to wear these things. Rather one could simply pull and twist and let things fall a little differently each time. In the middle of the room, there was a row of cabinets displaying jewelry. The pieces were delicate and bone-like, looking like casts of slim, broken branches or the molds of desert plants. These were not black, but white, the color of kaolin clay. Toward the back of the shop, I found, in one corner, a tailored suit of a black jacket and pants, made of soft wool, which I pulled out and showed to my mother and encouraged her to try on. When she came out and stood in front of the mirror, I noticed that the cut of the suit was not as shapeless as I had thought, but came in narrowly at the ribs, before flaring out slightly over the hips and thighs, the pants so loose and wide they were like French culottes. The effect was a carefully structured shape, much like the volumed silhouette of the Korean hanbok. I told my mother that it looked good on her, and it did. She could have been, in those garments, an entirely different person, anonymous and unplaceable.

On our last morning there, I took her to the Inari gates. It was cool and gray again, and we pulled on our puffer jackets and made our way through the little village of vendors and shrines and up toward the mountain. It had been raining overnight, and the path was wet and muddy. I asked her to be careful, to watch her step. I thought of how she had once told me that my great-grandfather had been a poet, and of all that was lost between that generation and ours.

As we walked, she asked me about my work. I didn't answer at first, and then I said that in many old paintings, one could discover what was called a pentimento, an earlier layer of something that the artist had chosen to paint over. Sometimes, these were as small as an object, or a color that had been changed, but other times, they could be as significant as a whole figure, an animal, or a piece of furniture. I said that in this way too, writing was just like painting. It was the only way that one could go back and change the past, to make things not as they were, but as we wished they had been, or rather as we saw it. I said, for this reason, it was better for her not to trust anything she read.

The further we went up the mountain, the more we left the crowds behind. The gates covered the paths and we passed under them. Some were a bright red, others a faded orange, their bases painted black. I had thought my mother would be tired, but she went up the steps without ever changing her pace, as if determined, or even angry. Soon, she was some way ahead of me. At several points, I stopped to rest. My legs still ached from the day before and my head was heavy. Before us, the gates went on at a gradual curve, fifteen degrees, ten, so that you were unable to fully see the way ahead of you, and you could not look back.

Eventually, we came out at a wooded slope, covered in blue-gray fern and cedar. I saw my mother standing near a large rock. I went up to her and got out my camera and adjusted the settings. I told her about a photographic series I had seen last year. Here, I said, the torii gates were preserved, a huge tourist site, but elsewhere, many older, smaller gates had been destroyed or abandoned. There had been, I recalled, a photo of an elegant structure strewn in a tropical forest. In another, one had been laid against a park bench, put aside for recycling. Then I took her hand in mine and clicked the shutter with the other. Later, looking back at the image, I could see that we were both not quite ready for the camera: weary, surprised and somehow very alike.

My mother went up to one of the little shops at the top of the mountain and we ordered green tea and something to eat. She bought a tiny charm, a white fox, and two postcards. I realized that everything she had bought here was a gift for someone else. The tea was hot and good, and the food small buns whose center contained a filling of sweet beans. We found a seat on a bench and looked out toward the view, watching as other tourists passed through the last of the gates looking either tired or bored, or climbed rocks in order to take photos of themselves and the valley beneath.

Before we had to head to the airport, we had a small amount of time to spare, and so we went to a shop in a converted temple. We separated again, as had become our habit, and I bought a blue scarf for Laurie, and some thick notepaper for myself with the last of my yen. When I had finished paying, I turned to look for my mother but could not see her in any of the sections. After a few minutes I found her waiting for me at the entrance, sitting on the bench, looking—and for all I knew this could have been the case—as if she had been there the whole time. The door made a frame of her against the outside, and she sat as a statue might have sat, with her hands folded peacefully in her lap and her knees and feet together, so that there was no part of her body that was not touching, and so that she could have been made out of a single stone. She had too the quality of a sculpture, and was breathing deeply, as if finally content. I pulled on my coat, and walked toward her around the people who were just entering. As I approached, she saw me and made a gesture with her hand. Could you help me with this? she said, and I saw that she was unable to bend down far enough to reach her shoe. I knelt and, with one swift tug, helped her pull it on.

Acknowledgments

With thanks to Ivor Indyk, Nick Tapper, Jacques Testard, Barbara Epler, Tynan Kogane, Clare Forster, Ian See, Emily Kiddell, Nicola Williams, Emily Fiske, and Louise Swinn.

With love and thanks to Celia, Oliver, Erin, Fi, and Pip.

About the author

Jessica Au is a writer based in Melbourne, Australia. *Cold Enough for Snow* won the inaugural Novel Prize, run by Giramondo, New Directions, and Fitzcarraldo Editions, and has been translated into over twelve languages.